"Um...would you like to take some pie with you? Can't eat it all, would hate to throw it out."

Matt smiled. A soft smile, barely visible through the scruff. Kelly duly—but not dully—considered that scruff, about how sensitive her skin was, and her heart started banging so hard she nearly passed out—

"Can't have that, God knows."

What? Oh. "No," she said. "Can't have that." Goodness *gracious,* her sternum was going to hurt like hell in the morning. "Well. Okay. Let me get that packed up for you...."

Kelly turned toward the kitchen, letting out a little gasp when she found herself somehow cradled to his chest.

Oh, she thought, smelling him, wanting to *inhale* him as she listened to his lovely strong heartbeat and soaked up how amazing those arms felt folded around her. She nearly cried, it felt so good and it had been so long, and heck, yeah, she missed this....

"Your call," he said, and Kelly did flinch.

"Wh-what?"

"Whether I go or stay." He smiled. "It's up to you."

* * *

JERSEY BOYS: Born...raised...and ready.

Dear Reader,

I'll admit it, I've always had a thing for those Tri-State guys, from Brooklyn or Long Island, Queens or New Jersey. The accent, the swagger, that unapologetically direct eye contact and those make-your-heart-stop grins...be still my heart. So casting them as heroes for my Jersey Boys series was a no-brainer...and loads of fun. Especially for the sassy, take-no-guff gals who eventually bring these dudes to their knees!

But my stories are also always about family, in the many ways that's defined these days—people living and loving and laughing together, whether by choice or happenstance. And for the grown Noble kids, most of whom are adopted, that might mean rethinking their pasts before they can accept whatever blessings the present might have to offer. Certainly that's true for the überprotective, and painfully divorced, Matt Noble, who wonders if he sees in his old high school crush Kelly McNeil a second chance—not only to be the husband the widow had only thought she was getting, but the father her children never really had....

Enjoy!

Karen Templeton

The Real Mr. Right

Karen Templeton

HARLEQUIN® SPECIAL EDITION®

Recycling programs for this product may not exist in your area.

ISBN-13: 978-0-373-65795-7

THE REAL MR. RIGHT

This edition published by arrangement with Harlequin Books S.A.

For questions and comments about the quality of this book, please contact us at CustomerService@Harlequin.com.

Printed in U.S.A.

Books by Karen Templeton

Harlequin Special Edition

§*Husband Under Construction* #2120
⌘*Fortune's Cinderella* #2161
¤*The Doctor's Do-Over* #2211
¤*A Gift for All Seasons* #2223
¤*The Marriage Campaign* #2242
§§*The Real Mr. Right* #2313

Silhouette Special Edition

***Baby Steps* #1798
***The Prodigal Valentine* #1808
***Pride and Pregnancy* #1821
Ω*Dear Santa* #1864
Ω*Yours, Mine...or Ours?* #1876
Ω*Baby, I'm Yours* #1893
§*A Mother's Wish* #1916
§*Reining in the Rancher* #1948
Ω*From Friends to Forever* #1988
§*A Marriage-Minded Man* #1994
§*Welcome Home, Cowboy* #2054
§*Adding Up to Marriage* #2073

Harlequin Romantic Suspense

Δ*Plain-Jane Princess* #1096
Δ*Honky-Tonk Cinderella* #1120
What a Man's Gotta Do #1195
Saving Dr. Ryan #1207
Fathers and Other Strangers #1244
Staking His Claim #1267
◆*Everybody's Hero* #1328
◆*Swept Away* #1357
◆*A Husband's Watch* #1407

Yours Truly

**Wedding Daze*
**Wedding Belle*
**Wedding? Impossible!*

**Babies, Inc.
ΔHow to Marry a Monarch
*Weddings, Inc.
◆The Men of Mayes County
ΩGuys and Daughters
§Wed in the West
⌘The Fortunes of Texas: Whirlwind Romance
¤Summer Sisters
§§Jersey Boys

Other titles by this author available in ebook format.

KAREN TEMPLETON

A recent inductee into the Romance Writers of America Hall of Fame, three-time RITA® award-winning author Karen Templeton has written more than thirty novels for Harlequin. She lives in New Mexico with two hideously spoiled cats, has raised five sons and lived to tell the tale, and could not live without dark chocolate, mascara and Netflix.

To all those amazing, selfless people
who open their homes,
their lives,
and their hearts
to other people's children
and call them "ours."

Bless you.

Chapter One

Her arm muscles screaming from the weight of the sacked-out toddler slumped against her chest, Kelly McNeil blinked up at the multigabled Queen Anne, so still and serene in the dark…and prayed she wasn't making the biggest mistake of her life.

Okay, the *second*-biggest mistake—

"Who'd you say these people were again?"

Behind her, the minivan's engine ticked itself to sleep, the sound overloud in the deep winter silence, and Kelly smiled briefly for her young son.

"This is where my best friend lived," she said, her heart knocking as they started up the softly lit brick walk that bisected the snow-shrouded front yard. "We'll be safe here."

Between the twin disks of his Harry Potter glasses, Cooper's nose scrunched. "You sure?"

"Yes," Kelly said, because she had to believe that or die. As it was, she felt as though she'd never be completely free of the fear knotting her stomach…a fear that had finally trampled her last shred of common sense. Because this was so not her, this was *insane,* uprooting two kids in the middle of the night and taking them someplace she hadn't even seen for nearly twenty years. She knew the Colonel still lived there, Sabrina had said so in her last Christmas letter, but his number was unlisted and Sabrina had apparently changed her cell phone number—

Swallowing hard, Kelly boosted Aislin higher on her shoulder and trudged up the steps to the porch, where brass coach lamps still stood sentry on either side of the glossy black door, illuminating the weathered gray floorboards, the dark green porch swing that had been privy to many a summer night's adolescent gripefest….

Blowing out a breath, Kelly pressed the doorbell. A dog barked. A big one, by the sound of it. Coop sidled closer.

"Dad—"

"Doesn't know where we are, sweetie."

"You sure?"

"Positive."

"How come?"

Because by the time she and Rick had met, her third year of college, her father was dead and her mother had moved to Philly and Maple River, New Jersey, had quietly slipped into her past. Oh, Sabrina had been one of Kelly's bridesmaids and had visited after Coop's birth, but there'd been no reason for Kelly to return here. "It never came up," she said quietly, and Coop nodded.

Except he then glanced over his shoulder, worried, and Kelly tugged him closer, fury hard-edging the fear. A moment later, through the frosted panels framing the door, a light flashed on. Sabrina wasn't there, of course—girlfriend had traded the Garden State 'burbs for Manhattan years before. And Bree's mom, Jeanne, had died some years before. Which left the Colonel. Who'd always scared Kelly a little, truth be told. Man hadn't risen through the ranks of the air force as quickly as he had by being a softie, that was for sure.

But for all Preston Noble's penchant for order and discipline, he'd also adored his five kids, four of whom were adopted. And Kelly had come to associate "next door" with love and laughter and the security that comes from being in a large family where everyone had each other's backs. Sure, Sabrina's dad might glower and bluster for a moment, especially at the late hour, but Kelly had no doubt he'd allow her and her children the same refuge he'd not only given to an untold number of foster kids over the years but also more rescue animals than she could count.

At least until she figured out what came next.

The door swung open; Kelly sucked in a breath...only to nearly choke when she realized the dark-haired, beard-hazed man hanging on to the excited bear of a dog wasn't the Colonel. The man frowned, confusion rampant in deep brown eyes even more intense than she remembered.

"Alf! Sit!" he commanded, glowering first at the dog, then her after the beast obeyed. "Can I help you?"

Clearly, he had no idea who she was. But even after eighteen years, Kelly would have recognized Sabrina's twin brother, Matt, anywhere.

Hell.

Behind owl-like glasses, embarrassment flared in the woman's oddly familiar green eyes as she cradled the baby's head to her shoulder. The chipmunk-cheeked boy beside her inched closer, the move belying the minute thrust to his chin. Wrong house would be Matt's guess.

Until she said, "Matt? It's...Kelly. Kelly Harrison. Mc-

Neil, I mean. Sabrina's old friend?" And he felt like he'd been sucker punched.

Holy crap. When was the last time he'd even thought about Kelly McNeil—?

She cleared her throat. "Is…is your dad here?"

"Uh, no." Unable to contain herself at the sight of the boy, Alf surged to her feet again; Matt tightened his hold on her collar until butt once again touched floor. "Actually, he's out of town."

"Oh. Well. Um… Sorry for bothering you." Kelly touched the boy's shoulder. "Come on, Coop—"

"No, it's okay," Matt said, confused as hell but not about to send a woman and two kids back out in subfreezing weather. "Please…come in." He opened the door wider, kneeing aside the whimpering Newfoundland. When Kelly hesitated, Matt sighed. "Really. And don't mind Alf, she's harmless. Although you might want to watch out for slobber."

That got a pair of tiny smiles, before, with a murmured "Thanks," Kelly ushered the boy inside. Matt shouldered shut the heavy door as the draft sideswiped the thermostat, kicking it on. The kid—Coop—immediately hunkered in front of the brass floor register, the concerned dog standing guard, while Kelly lowered herself and the sleeping toddler to the painted bench in the foyer. Unbuttoning the top button to her own coat, she released a long breath. "That feels *so* good. The heat I mean. The heater's wonky in my car, and it took longer to get here than I'd expected."

"From?"

"Haleysburg," she said, naming a town about a half-hour's drive away. Her face reddened. "I don't want to put you out—"

"You're not."

"If you're sure," she whispered, her eyes drifting closed,

and he realized this clearly exhausted woman was not the same stuck-up girl who wouldn't give his sorry-assed self the time of day all those years ago. Still, an explanation might be nice right about now.

"Your kids, I take it?"

Kelly jerked, her eyes popping open. "Yes, sorry. I'm..." Yawning, she yanked off her white knit hat, freeing a billion red curls. Barely past her shoulders now. Not as bright. "This is Aislin. And that's Cooper. Coop?" The boy pushed upright, grabbing the dog's ruff to steady himself. "This is Matt Noble. My best friend's brother."

Coop seemed to gather himself before sticking out his hand. "Pleased to meet you," he said, like he was sixty, for God's sake, and Matt felt a smile elbow through his not-exactly-chipper mood.

"Pleased to meet you, too, Cooper." Not much of Kelly in the boy that he could see. Except for the curls, maybe, although they were brown. The set to his chin, however—that was Kelly all the way.

"Can I go in there?" he said, looking toward the living room, still crammed with Matt's mother's sometimes bizarre Americana collection.

"Sure. Knock yourself out."

As boy and dog wandered off, Kelly fingered back the baby's snowsuit hood to stroke her damp, strawberry-blond curls off her face. "I apologize for showing up out of the blue like this, but Sabrina must've changed her number and I'd forgotten the one here...." Her chin wobbled, steadied again. "And I was...desperate."

Matt's eyes narrowed. "You in some kind of trouble?" he asked, giving voice to the question that'd been poking him between the eyes from the moment he laid eyes on her. Because you can take the cop off the force, but taking the force out of the cop—not so easy.

Kelly's mouth turned down at the corners. "Not sure that's the right word. My ex—"

The toddler suddenly jolted awake, huge blue eyes assessing Matt for a moment before swerving to her mother.

"Mama—?"

"It's okay, baby," Kelly whispered, smiling for her little girl, a smile like Matt remembered her giving to anybody but him back in the day, and something *pinged* in the pit of his stomach. The kind of *pinging* lonely, divorced schlubs would do well to ignore.

"Your ex-what?"

Except then Cooper and Alf reappeared, and Kelly shook her head, color once more flooding her cheeks. And finally it clicked, what would make a woman drag two kids out in the middle of the night, to someplace she hadn't been in years. True, there weren't any obvious signs, no black eyes or visible bruises, but—

"You guys want something to eat?" he asked, tamping down a repulsion that had never faded, even after nearly thirty years, and Kelly's grateful smile cracked his heart. Because the past had nothing to do with *now*.

And *now* she obviously needed his help.

Whether he was totally on board with that idea or not.

Kelly sat at the glittery white quartz island, Aislin pitched forward on her lap to smush pudgy little fingers into the sparklies, thinking that, on the one hand, the heat purring through the register and the smell of browned butter as Matt made grilled-cheese sandwiches—under the dog's unwavering supervision—were soothingly familiar. Enough that Kelly felt her perpetually tight shoulder muscles unknot. A little.

Because what was also familiar—and not soothing in the least—was her wack-a-doo reaction to this dude she hadn't seen since she was sixteen. An eon, practically, during which she'd fallen in love, married, become a mom twice over. As in, moved on?

And yet…

True, she was worn-out, and emotionally trashed, and time had definitely blessed Matteo Noble, who hadn't exactly been shabby before. On him, that whole dark, moody, broody thing worked. It was how it was all working on *her* that was seriously messing with her already fritzed brain.

So, no. Not going there.

Instead she ruffled Coop's hair as he sat next to her, staring up at the assorted copper cookware hanging off a rack, and corralled her wayward thoughts as she gave the renovated kitchen a once-over. Gone were the knotty pine cupboards, the beat-up, trampoline-size maple table where the island now stood, the brick-patterned linoleum. Now it was all very HGTV, stainless steel, glass-tile backsplash and pale wood floor. Very nice, very generic. Very not Matt's mom, an energetic little blonde who'd always been far too busy feeding people to worry about her kitchen's décor.

As if reading her mind, Matt said, "We talked Dad into a remodel a few months. Since he's making noises about wanting to sell the house, anyway, and eighties nostalgia wasn't gonna cut it."

Remembering that their mother had died several years before, Kelly gently asked, "How's he doing?"

Matt flipped the sandwiches on the griddle. Shrugged. "He functions. Putters. Reads. Sometimes hangs out at Tyler and Abby's salvage shop—Sabrina tell you about that?"

"Briefly, yes. How's that going?"

"Good. Restoration's a hot market these days. So's repurposing. It's amazing, the stuff they pull out of old buildings. Not to mention who buys it. This one guy, he completely refaced the outside of his house with bricks from a demolished factory in Trenton. Nuts, right?"

What was nuts was how they were shooting the breeze as though it hadn't been a million years since they'd seen each other. As though things hadn't been painfully awkward between them, especially at the end.

And that was the smaller of the two elephants in the room. The far larger, stinkier one was the big old "why?" that was behind her bringing the kids here.

Especially since she knew Matt was a cop. A detective, if memory served. So this reprieve—because of the kids, the hour—would undoubtedly be short-lived. At some point there would be questions. Questions Matt had every right to ask. Not that his dad wouldn't have expected explanations, too, but she'd always felt she could trust the Colonel to protect her, the same way he'd protected his own children. Not to mention all those foster kids he and Jeanne had taken in over the years.

But Matt... This was uncharted territory. Yes, he was feeding them and being chatty—he'd been raised right—but could she count on him to take her side? To even believe her—?

"You got awfully quiet," Matt said, scattering her thoughts.

"It's been a long...day."

His forehead wrinkled for a moment before he said, with a wink for Aislin, "Almost done."

Her eyes stinging, Kelly pulled her baby closer, burying her cheek in her silky curls. Thank God this one seemed unaffected by the events of the past two years. The same, however, couldn't be said for Cooper, who leaned heavily on the counter as he watched Matt, smushed face propped in hand. Yawning, he shoved up his glasses to rub his eyes, and Kelly's heart turned over. Poor guy was probably dead on his feet.

"They can bunk in Tyler's old room when they're done," Matt said. "There's twin beds—"

"Oh. I brought sleeping bags—"

"No need." Matt's gaze touched hers, then slid to Coop as he cut the finished sandwiches in quarters, clunked the plates onto the counter. "Whaddya want to drink, sport? Juice? Milk?" He grinned. "*Chocolate* milk?"

"Mom?" he said, hopeful eyed, and she smiled.

"For tonight? Sure."

Coop sat up straighter and nodded. "Yes, please. Thank you."

She bit her lip, though, when Matt retrieved a carton of one percent milk, a container of "skinny" chocolate syrup from the stainless-steel French-door fridge. He threw her a glance. "Dad's stuff. Doctor's orders."

"Oh! Is he okay?"

"Yeah, he's fine...." He rummaged in a cupboard for something. "Probably healthier than I am. Doc wants him to *stay* healthy, though. Ah—I knew I'd seen one of these...."

Moments later, he'd rinsed out and poured milk into someone's old sippy cup, which he then handed to Aislin, who plugged it into her mouth and started chugging as though she hadn't had anything to drink in weeks. Matt chuckled, twin creases gouging those bearded cheeks, then turned that grin to Kelly, reminding her exactly how messed up her life was.

How messed up *she* was. Ergh.

"Linnie! What do you say?"

There was an actual popping sound when spout left mouth. "Thank you."

"You're welcome, sweetheart," Matt said, then faced Kelly again. "What about you?"

"I'll have what they're having," she said, watching Matt's strong hands as he poured her milk, noting how those hands were attached to equally strong arms, which in turn were attached to a good, solid chest, and for a brief moment, because she was crazy stressed, most likely, she imagined herself wrapped up in those arms, against that strong chest. And this wasn't even about sex—seriously, the very thought made her tired—but…caring. Being cared about—

"You want something else?" he asked, and her eyes jerked to his.

"What?"

"Your sandwich. You haven't touched it."

"Oh…sorry. No, this is fine, I'm just…" *About to cry. Great.* "I'm almost too tired to eat."

"I can see that," he said, being kind again, dammit. "By the way, you can take Sabrina's room—"

"Mom? I'm done. C'n we go play with the dog?"

Matt chuckled. "Mutt thought you'd never ask. Here—" he handed Cooper the plastic plate with the mangled remains of Aislin's sandwich "—go on into the family room, back there," he said, pointing. "Make her sit first, though. She knows the drill."

Kids and dog gone, Kelly finally took a bite of her sandwich. "This is really good."

"You must be really hungry."

She almost smiled. "You use butter?"

"Mom would reach down from heaven and smack me if I didn't."

Kelly bit off another corner, washed it down with the best chocolate milk ever. "Your mom used to make grilled-cheese sandwiches for Bree and me almost every day after school. You learned well."

Matt hesitated, then carted the griddle over to the sink. His back to her, he said, "Only thing my folks ever wanted was for any kid who set foot in this house to feel safe." He turned. "Making grilled-cheese sandwiches wasn't the only thing I learned well. So what's going on, Kelly?"

And there it was. She set down her milk glass, skimming her index finger over the damp rim before lifting her eyes to his. "Let me get the kids to bed first?"

He crossed his arms, doing the narrow-eyed thing again, and a shiver traipsed up her spine. Finally he walked back to the island and leaned heavily on the counter's edge, close enough for her to see the beginnings of crow's feet fanning from nearly black eyes.

"It's obvious you need help," he said, too softly for the kids to hear. "Which for old time's sake I'm more than willing to give you...but only if you swear to tell me everything. And I mean *everything.* So. Deal?"

"How do I know I can trust you?"

One side of his mouth kicked up. "You got any other options?"

She sighed. "Not really, no."

Still gripping the counter's edge, Matt straightened again, his gaze drifting to the kids in the family room before resettling on hers. "I may not share the Colonel's DNA, but I'm still his son. If you can count on him, you can count on me."

And God help her, she believed him. Because, as he so accurately pointed out, what choice did she have?

A half hour later, Matt lay sprawled in his dad's recliner, half watching some late-night TV show, when Kelly appeared in the room's entryway. He glanced over and his breath hitched in his chest.

She looked downright shrunken, hunched into herself as she distractedly rubbed one forearm with her other hand. Even as a teenager she'd been on the skinny side, but now, even with the baggy sweatshirt, she was all points and angles. Damn, her cheekbones had never been *that* sharp.

Or her eyes that flat.

"I was beginning to think you'd chickened out," he said. "Or passed out."

A weary smile touched her lips. Granted, Kelly hadn't been your typical, in-your-face Jersey girl—in fact, her being so quiet was what had first attracted him. But this went way beyond being reserved. Or stuck-up, which Matt now realized was absurd. No, the word that came to mind now was…*deflated.* Like the minute she didn't have to put up a front for her kids, she'd surrendered to whatever hell she was going through.

"I'd've never been able to sleep," she said, "knowing you were out here…wondering."

Matt clicked off the TV and levered the chair back upright. "You got that right—"

"Please don't feel obligated because you happened to be here instead of your dad."

"And I'm going to pretend I didn't hear that. I'm a cop, I took an oath to protect and serve, okay? Don't recall it saying I got to pick and choose who I protected."

"So…this isn't personal?"

"Not sure how it could be, since we haven't seen each other in, what? Nearly twenty years?"

"Got it." Then her brows pushed together. "Why are you here, anyway?"

He almost laughed. "Because why would I still be living with my father?"

"I didn't say—"

"But you *thought.* And are you gonna stand there the rest of the night or what?"

"I might."

For a split second, annoyance prickled. Until Matt realized that tiny, defiant act was her trying to keep some control over a situation in which she probably felt pretty damn powerless. So he leaned back in the chair, plucked his soda can from the holder on the chair's arm.

"My own house is all torn up at the moment," he said, taking a swig. "Okay, for longer than that. I'm doing most of the work myself so the remodel's not exactly going like gangbusters. No heat, no indoor plumbing.... You get the picture. So I'm camping out here."

She folded her arms over her stomach. "Sabrina mentioned your divorce. I'm sorry."

Even after nearly a year, the sting still took him by surprise. "Thanks," he said, appreciating her solicitude but having no intention of talking about his pulverized marriage. With her or anybody—

"So you're here alone?" she said.

"No, Abby's here, too." Matt jabbed a finger toward the ceiling. "Upstairs. She was up this morning at five, hit the hay before it was even nine. Another reason why I'm here, since Pop didn't much cotton to the idea of her being here alone."

"My goodness, how old is she now? Twenty?"

"Twenty-two. And pissed as all get-out that I'm here, cramping her style."

"Oh, and like the Colonel doesn't?"

Well, look at that. Was that an actual twinkle in those pretty green eyes? Matt chuckled. "Yeah, but I'm her brother. Which is far worse. Especially since Pop spoils her rotten."

"Don't give me that," Kelly said, still smiling. Sorta. "I remember how you guys were when she was little. You *all* spoiled her rotten."

"Maybe. Maybe not," he said, and Kelly laughed softly, then glanced toward the ceiling.

"I can't believe we didn't wake her up. She must sleep like the dead."

"She does. Always has. Last summer? Kid slept through a thunderstorm that sounded like it was gonna take out half the town." Alf shoved herself to her feet and padded over to Matt for some loving. He messed with the dog's ears for a moment or two, then frowned back at Kelly. "So. This story…?"

She cupped the back of her neck, her forehead creased. "You realize I can only give you my side?"

"Better than no side."

"And if I sound completely delusional?"

"Guess that's a risk you'll have to take." He took another swallow of the nearly flat soda. "But I somehow doubt your ex is buried in the woods somewhere."

"Thanks for the vote of confidence," Kelly said drily, then finally sat on the very edge of the sofa, jerking a limp red curl behind her ear. Her mouth pressed flat for a moment before she said, very softly, "I'm scared."

Point to him. "For you? The kids—?"

"Both."

"Your ex hurt you?" When her eyes shot to his, he said, "You started to say something. Earlier."

"Right." She blew a short, humorless laugh through her nose. "Depends on how you define *hurt*."

Matt released a slow, controlled breath. "You have custody?"

Nodding, she rubbed her hands against her jeans. "Except Rick is not happy about that. At all. Sure, he has visitation, but more and more he keeps showing up unannounced to see the kids. At first I let it go, thinking at least it showed he cared. That he's trying." Her mouth thinned again. "But even before tonight, it was unsettling. For the kids, I mean. Well, me, too..."

She mashed her lips together. "The frustration, the hurt, the anger—I understand that. Rick has every right to be disappointed. To be bitter. Hey, I'm pretty bitter and disappointed, too. I did love him," she said, her eyes filling. "With all my heart. But the day came when I realized that love alone wasn't enough to fix our broken marriage."

If it was one thing Matt had learned in his work, it was that one rarely got a straight shot at the truth, that more likely than not there'd be a few side trips along the way. But without those side trips, you were likely to miss something crucial. "Broken how?"

Kelly leaned back, grabbing a throw off the sofa's arm to wrap up in. "We met in college. Dated for... Gosh. Four or five years before we got engaged. Didn't get married for another year after that. Certainly long enough that I felt pretty sure Rick was, well, normal. He was... He made me feel secure. Safe. Like..." She sighed. "Like my dad used to. Over and over, Rick assured me that I could lean on him, that's what he was there for.

"And he was a good provider. A good dad. We were happy. For a while, anyway. He is—or at least was—a gifted salesman. And I was good with being a stay-at-home mom. I even liked my in-laws," she said with a flicker of a smile. "Except, when...when Aislin was about six months old, Rick lost his job. And another one didn't exactly land in his lap. I'd been doing a few small catering jobs here and there—mostly friends of his parents, that sort of thing—so I figured that was as good a time as any to expand. I had a little money, from my dad's life insurance policy, so I invested it in my business." Alf switched allegiances, chuffing over to rest her chin on Kelly's knee. She smiled, plowing her fingers through the dog's thick fur. "It blossomed, more than I could've dreamed. But Rick..."

Her hand fisted. "Instead of supporting my work—which was keeping us from losing the house—he resented my success. I don't doubt," she quickly added, "that his pride had taken a huge hit, that he was hurting because he couldn't keep his promise to provide for us. Having watched my father go through the same thing when he got sick, I understood that. But..."

Kelly folded her legs underneath her to prop her elbows on her knees, leaning her head in her hands. "I didn't want a divorce. Not for a long time. Especially after Rick's father died and I didn't want to cause him any more pain. And in any case, I kept thinking—" dropping her hands, she sighed "—that this was one of those 'or worse' times and that somehow, we'd work through it. He was my *husband,* Matt," she said at Matt's pissed sigh, briefly meeting his gaze. "The man I'd promised to love no matter what..."

For a moment, she seemed to disappear inside herself, then said, very softly, "And it wasn't as if we hadn't weathered rough patches before. Except then," she said on another sigh, "Rick started drinking more than usual. And his behavior became more...irrational. He'd either fly off the handle over nothing—especially to Coop, who he'd pick on mercilessly—or sink into this bottomless depression that was almost worse than the anger. And when Coop's grades started to slip, when he started overeating..."

A sad smile preceded what she said next. "I finally told Rick it was over, I was done trying to hold our marriage together single-handedly. But until I actually handed him the divorce papers I'm sure he thought I was bluffing."

"How long ago was this?"

"Almost three years." Her eyes filled. "And despite everything, it broke my heart. Even though, yes, I've finally accepted that whatever's going on in Rick's head has nothing to do with me. But on some level—" another sigh "—it still kills me that I couldn't figure out how to fix things."

Yeah. He knew how that went, didn't he? Knew, too, the folly of that particular mind-set, thinking if one person wants things to work badly enough, it can happen. "And sometimes, the only way to fix something *is* to walk away."

Silence shuddered between them for several beats before, on a long breath, she sagged back into the couch. "Yeah. I know." Her eyes lowered to the dog's ginormous head, still on her lap. "Except the divorce didn't end the… problems."

"The drinking, you mean?"

"That, and the emotional outbursts. If anything, they got worse." Kelly lifted her eyes again, and the fear Matt saw there knifed him in the gut. "In fact, Rick's only supposed to be with the kids when his mother's around. Since he lives with her now."

"Are you okay with that?"

"Very. I'd trust Lynn with my life. And my kids'. She's devastated by what's happened. And as frustrated at not being able to get through to Rick as I was. Am. So this seemed a reasonable compromise. Except, as I said, he keeps coming over. And about a week ago, I noticed this… blankness in his eyes. And that…"

Her lower lip briefly quivered. "I've tried talking to Family Services to get a restraining order but they don't issue those on hunches. On *feelings.* On things that…" Pressing her lips together, she gave her head a quick shake. "On what *might* happen. And since he's never actually harmed the children…"

Something in her voice… Matt's eyes narrowed. "So what changed things?"

A moment or two passed before she said, "Rick called, long after the kids were asleep, wanting to talk to Coop. I said no and he went ballistic. More than usual, I mean. Then he insinuated…" She swallowed. "He said if he c-couldn't have the kids whenever he wanted, then neither of us could."

Matt froze. "And you took that to mean…?"

"Something I can't even think about. And what really scared me was that he wasn't drunk. Not that I could tell, anyway."

For several seconds, Matt stared at her profile as she kept her gaze fixed on the coffee table between them. He would never have figured the Kelly he'd once known for a liar—Sabrina wouldn't have kept her as a friend if she had been. But he didn't know this Kelly, did he? "You think he was serious?"

She lifted tear-filled eyes to Matt again. If she *was* pulling one over on him, she was doing a bang-up job. "I sure wasn't going to stick around and find out, was I? Court orders be damned." She sighed. "So. Here we are. Still want to help me?"

Matt sat forward, like that would relieve the agita. In theory he understood the impossibility of mitigating every potential nightmare. No police force in the country had those kinds of resources. Also, in theory, as an officer of the law he was bound to uphold that law. And for God's sake, not be a party to someone breaking that law.

Except he'd also seen firsthand how often inaction led to unimaginable horror. And even more unimaginable grief. Maybe he couldn't say for sure she was telling the truth, but his gut told him she was. At least, mostly. Because his gut was also telling him she was holding something back. Something he'd pry out of her later, for sure.

But not tonight.

After a long moment Matt got to his feet and looked past Kelly into the kitchen. "You sure nobody can connect you to this place? Your ex? His mother?"

"Positive."

"But they can contact you?"

"They have my cell number, yes. And no, it can't be traced. I checked."

He almost smiled. "I couldn't—and won't—even try to advise you on what to do. In fact—" he finally met her gaze "—this conversation? Never happened. Got it?"

A frown momentarily dug into her brow, then eased. "Yes."

"Then you can stay here, at least for the moment. Until you—we—figure something out. I'm sure Dad would agree. And in any case, he won't be back for a week. By that time… Well. Anything can happen, right?"

Kelly stood and shoved her hair away from her face. "And Abby?"

He'd forgotten about his sister. Crap.

"Tell her whatever you think seems best. People come through here all the time. She probably won't think anything one way or the other."

"But you're still putting your butt on the line."

"True. But so are you."

"Why?" she said softly, and he knew what she was asking.

"Frankly? I have no idea."

Kelly blinked a couple times, then crossed the floor to put her hands on his shoulders, standing on tiptoe to kiss his cheek. "Thank you," she whispered, then padded out of the room, leaving Matt pretty sure he wasn't going to sleep worth crap tonight.

Chapter Two

When Kelly's phone buzzed at some ungodly hour the next morning, she checked the display, then stiffened. However, tempting as it was to let the call go through to voice mail, she knew Rick would only keep calling until she answered. More than once, she'd considered getting a new number. But even as messed up as things had been, she still hadn't been able to completely cut him off. Not that she could have, anyway, with the kids.

After last night, however...

Still dressed, she unwrapped herself from the heavy Pendleton blanket that had been folded at the foot of Sabrina's bed and crunched forward, forking her fingers through her tangled curls before answering.

"Where the hell are you?" Rick said.

Meaning he'd been by the apartment. Squeezing her eyes shut, Kelly hugged the brightly patterned blanket to her cramping chest, reminding herself of how far she'd come, that she was brave and strong and no longer vulnerable to Rick's guilt trips. To his threats, veiled or otherwise. That she was nobody's victim, dammit. "You don't need to know that right now."

"The hell you say. And that's not answering the question."

Anger propelled her off the bed, even if she did cling to the bedpost for support as she shoved her still-socked feet into her sneakers. "Yes, it is—"

"It's not right, Kelly," Rick whined in her ear, "not knowing where my kids are. Why are you punishing me like this?"

Dear God—was he *serious?* She sank onto the edge of the rumpled bed, her free arm strangling her trembling stomach. Had she dreamed last night? Or misinterpreted things that badly?

Then she remembered his voice, low and cold, uttering words she would have never dreamed she'd ever hear come out of his mouth, even at his worst, and her strength returned. "This isn't about punishing you, it's about protecting our children—"

"That's bull—"

"You threatened them, Rick!" she whispered, praying the kids were still asleep. "Said if you couldn't have them, then neither of us could."

"*What?* Where the hell are you getting this?"

"From you. Word for word."

A beat or two passed before he said, "Even if I did say that, you've got it all balled up, I couldn't have possibly meant—"

"I know what I heard, Rick. And how you said it. You telling me you don't remember—?"

"I don't, swear to God. Whether you believe me or not."

Kelly sighed so hard it was almost painful. "Well, you

did. Whether you believe *me* or not. Look, I know we've had this conversation a hundred times already, but I'm going to say it again—*you need help.* And if what went down last night doesn't bring that home for you, I don't know what will. And until you get that help—" she fisted her free hand "—I'm not letting you anywhere near the kids. End of discussion, I'm done."

Shaking slightly, she disconnected the call as Matt appeared at the open bedroom door, startling her, his arms crossed as if nothing short of a tornado would budge him. While she probably looked like a headlight-blinded possum a split second before *splat.*

Wondering how much he'd heard—and deciding she didn't care—Kelly splayed her fingers through her hair again, then let her hand drop.

"Kind of hard to have a meltdown with you gawking at me like that."

"You think I've never seen a meltdown before?"

"Not from me you haven't. And trust me, it's not pretty."

"Somehow, I doubt you can top Sabrina in that department—"

"Matt! For heaven's sake—don't you have someplace, anyplace, to be?"

He shoved his fingers into his jeans' pockets, revealing a dark green corduroy shirt underneath a beat-up leather jacket. Black, of course. To go with the beard stubble, even more pronounced than it'd been last night. "Yeah, actually," he said on a rush of air, "I'm expecting a delivery at the house, then I'm headed into the city. But it can wait—"

"No. Really. We'll be fine." Kelly tried to smile, failed, went with a frustrated growl instead. "Dammit—I thought I'd feel relieved once we got away. Instead I feel… I don't know. Like…like maybe I overreacted."

Matt's expression darkened. "And what was the alternative? Stick around until something bad did happen? Like you said yourself, sometimes you gotta listen to that voice."

"Then why can't I trust that? If it's so right, why am I second-guessing myself?" Her hand shot up. "Never mind, don't answer that. Not that you could. And, anyway, you don't need to get sucked into this any more than you already are. But thanks. For letting us stay here."

"No problem," Matt said, then extended his hand. "Give me your phone."

She pressed it to her chest. "Why?"

"So I can plug in my number, why do you think? And I want yours, too." When she hesitated, he pushed out a breath. "I'm not gonna stalk you, for God's sake. Just give me the damn phone." So she did, and watched with the strangest mixture of relief and worry as he deftly added his number to her contacts. "You need anything, you call, you hear me? And before you give me any this-is-my-problem-not-yours crap… I get that, okay? Doesn't mean you have to deal with it alone." He handed back her phone, then dug his out of his jacket pocket. Waited.

She sighed, told him then frowned. "Why are you being so nice to me? I mean, for all intents and purposes we're strangers—"

"Like hell." Matt slipped his phone back into his pocket, then slammed his hands into his jacket pockets. "I mean, yeah, on the surface, you have a point. But we saw each other nearly every day for years. That hardly makes us strangers. In fact, I'm guessing both Sabrina and my dad would say you were family. Not to mention my mom, if she were still here. And they'd all three wring my neck if they thought I'd left you to swing in the breeze. So deal with it."

She almost smiled. "Is there another option?"

"No." He started to leave, turned back. "Abby should be up soon, the dog's already been out and everything's fair game in the kitchen. I'll be back by two, but if you need anything—"

"Yeah, yeah, got it. Thanks."

He gave her a long, disquieting look, then huffed out a breath. "Just so you know? I'm not entirely unconflicted about this. Like you said, I've only got your side of the story. That said, I've worked my fair share of domestic abuse cases, saw more times than I can count women who *didn't* follow their instincts, who either didn't see or didn't want to see the warning signs. Or were too scared to act on them. So if what you're saying is true…then what you're doing? Takes balls."

With that, he finally left. Only somehow his presence remained, all that *uber*macho protective energy vibrating around her. Through her. And she thought, *This is bad.*

Because what she had brewing here was a perfect storm of overwrought, celibate woman colliding with honorable hunk…to whom, alas, Kelly wasn't *less* attracted than she had been in days of yore.

So, yeah. Hell.

By rights, she should have felt more safe, more secure, that Matt took his protective role so seriously, his justified ambivalence notwithstanding. He'd keep her babies safe, and that was all that mattered. And God knew it would be so easy to simply…let go, let someone else do the thinking, the planning, the worrying.

Except leaning on men—her father, then Rick… She'd done that her entire life. Until that support got ripped away and she'd nearly drowned in her own insecurities.

A ragged breath left Kelly's mouth as she squatted to dig clean clothes out of the jumbled mess inside her suitcase. She wasn't stupid. And heaven knew if pride had been an issue she wouldn't even be here. But there was a fine line between knowing when to ask for help and expecting other people to fix your problems for you. Having barely figured out the difference, for damn sure she wasn't about to slip back into old habits. Not just for her sake, but especially for her children's.

Meaning as much as the old Kelly ached to let Matt be Matt, the new one didn't dare.

Showered and dressed in at least a clean variation of what she'd worn the day before, Kelly checked on her still-sleeping children before following the heady aroma of brewing coffee to the kitchen. By now the sun had hauled its butt up over the horizon, blasting the space with light and making the countertops glisten more than the patchy snow outside. Matt, bless his heart, had made enough coffee for half the town, and Kelly gratefully filled the huge mug sitting by the maker.

She took that first, glorious sip and sighed. Amazing, what a shower, sunshine and a shot of caffeine could do to brighten one's mood. Or at least make one feel…hopeful. What tomorrow—shoot, the next hour—would bring, she had no idea. But right now things were better than they had been last night. And that she could work with.

The Newfie clicked over to the French doors, parked her big old nose against one of the panes and rolled back one eye. "No," Kelly said, and, with a heavy sigh, the dog lumbered off to plop down in a pool of sunlight. Wow. If only the kids were that easy to wrangle.

Inside her jeans' pocket, her phone vibrated in tandem with her mother-in-law's ringtone, and the hopefulness wavered.

"Hi, Lynn," she said softly, searching for something, anything, the kids would eat, since her cooking skills were totally lost on them.

"You really took the kids away?"

Lucky Charms! Yes! "I really did."

"Far?"

"Far enough. Doubt Rick and I will run into each other in the supermarket." An unlikely possibility, in any case, since Rick hadn't seen the inside of a grocery store in decades. She unearthed a pair of plastic bowls from the cupboard, set them on the counter.

"Why now?"

Kelly leaned against the counter, her heart hammering as she squinted into the sun pouring into the formal dining room through two sets of French doors. Since the last thing Kelly wanted to do was add to Lynn's pain, she'd refused to gripe to the woman about her son, either before or after the divorce. Now was no different. One day, maybe, she'd tell her…everything. But not this morning. So a little fudging was in order. "Because, for one thing, he keeps showing up drunk—"

"Showing up where? To your place?"

"Yes."

"When the kids are there?"

"That would be his point, unfortunately. And when he's drunk he's…not a nice person And last night he called—really late—and he got pretty…belligerent. And I just felt we needed to get away. At least for a while."

"Without telling Rick where you went?"

"Yes."

A moment's pause preceded Lynn's quiet comment. "So what you're saying is he's getting worse."

The despair in the older woman's voice seared Kelly's insides. "I'm so sorry, Lynn, I know this must feel like I'm punishing you, too—"

"And why should you be sorry? This isn't your fault."

Kelly swallowed, trying to ease the thickness in her throat. "I was afraid you wouldn't believe me."

"For God's sake, sweetheart… I do have two eyes in my head. Okay, maybe I had a hard time at first, accepting the truth—what mother wants to believe her own son could turn into…" Kelly heard Lynn take a shaky breath, and tears welled in her own eyes. "Into s-somebody she doesn't even recognize anymore. But I saw how hard you fought to keep your marriage together. And frankly, if it'd been me in the same situation? I don't know if I could've held out as long as you did."

Her former mother-in-law's kindness nearly did her in. And only further muddled the whole sordid mess.

"Thank you," Kelly whispered, and Lynn made a sound that was half laugh, half sigh.

"For what?"

"Being…you."

That got a snort. "Like I'm going to be somebody else? So maybe this'll be the kick in the pants Ricky needs. Maybe one day—soon, God willing—he'll pull his head out of his butt and see what he's doing, get back on track. And who knows? Maybe the two of you could work things out—"

"Lynn. Please…don't."

Another sigh. "I know. It's just… I want you to be happy, sweetheart. For all of us to be happy again. Like we used to be. That's not such a bad thing, is it?"

Finally, Kelly picked up the box of cereal, started to pour it into the bowls. "Not a bad thing at all. And I won't keep the kids from you, I promise—"

"Hey. That's mine."

At the young woman's Jersey-tough voice, Kelly dropped the box, sending little marshmallow and sugary oat bits skittering across the kitchen floor and the dog into a feeding frenzy. Wresting the box from underneath the Newfie's elephant-size paw, she heard Lynn say, "Okay,

I gotta get going. But you call me anytime, okay? I love you, baby—"

The person attached to the voice clomped across the floor, snatched the box off the counter. Glowered at Kelly. Who pointed to her phone, then said into it, "I love you, too, Lynn."

"I know, honey. I know."

Her chest aching, Kelly disconnected the call and slipped her phone into her pocket, then faced the wiry little blonde in jeans, hoodie and a scraped-back ponytail who probably didn't weigh as much as Coop. Without makeup, she looked about twelve. And yet, as Kelly watched Abby dump cereal into a bowl and clomp back toward the island—in a pair of the ugliest work boots on God's green earth—she decided in a barroom brawl, her money was on the pipsqueak.

"Abby?" she said, even though Kelly would have known her anywhere, she looked exactly like her mother. If leaner and meaner.

"That's me, yep." The bowl set, Matt's sister veered back toward the coffeemaker, only to glare at the mug in Kelly's hand. Oops.

"Matt told me to help myself to anything, I didn't realize the cereal was yours—"

"And the mug."

"O-kay! Here, I'll find something else—"

"Fuggedaboutit." Twisting her ponytail in her hand, Abby slammed open a cupboard door, grabbed another mug. Banged the door shut hard enough to make things rattle. Opened the fridge, grabbed milk, slammed that door, too.

"Um… I take it you're not a morning person—?"

One hand shot up, cutting her off. The other poured her coffee, lifted the mug to her mouth. Two, three sips later,

Abby let her head loll back, her eyes drift shut. She opened them again, took another swallow then sighed.

"Sorry. I'm a bear before my coffee."

"I can relate. I'm Kelly, by the way."

"Yeah. Matt texted me, told me you and your kids were here." She made a face. "That I should be nice." Abby turned, smushing her skinny little butt against the edge of the counter. "Like that's even an issue, I'm always nice."

Kelly smiled. "So you don't remember me?" At the young woman's head shake, Kelly said, "Your sister and I were best friends. I remember when you were born. In fact, I used to change your stinky diapers."

She took another swallow. "Gross."

"It's okay, you were so cute we didn't mind."

Snorting, Abby carted her mug back to the island, climbed onto a stool and poured milk over her cereal. Shoveled in a bite. Something felt slightly off, but Kelly couldn't quite put her finger on what. That Abby sounded and acted a little young for her age, maybe? Then again, did Kelly even remember what twenty-two sounded like anymore?

"I do sorta remember you," Abby said, a smile finally appearing as she chewed. "You and Bree used to let me watch stuff Mom and Daddy would've had a fit about if they'd known."

"Did we scar you for life?"

For a moment, a shadow dimmed the smile. "No," Abby said quietly, then dispatched another bite of cereal. Chewing slowly, the blonde sat back, arms folded over her flat chest, her gaze questioning and astute, and Kelly instantly recognized the childish act for what it was—an act. Girl was sharp as a tack. Sharp enough, most likely, to see through any truth dodging on Kelly's part. Especially when she asked, "So why are you here? I mean, when's the last time you saw any of us?"

"It's been a while. But I'm still in touch with Sabrina. Sort of."

"Who doesn't live here. Which I assume you know."

Kelly blew out a breath, then refilled her coffee mug. Obviously Matt's text hadn't been elucidating. "Just needed a break, that's all."

"From?"

Her shoulders bumped. "Life," she said, and Abby's eyes narrowed. Exactly like Matt's—a thought that brought on a brief, though piquant, shudder—even though they weren't related by blood. Except then, with a shrug, Abby slanted forward again to resume eating.

"Hey, I don't know you, got no reason to get up in your business." She swallowed, then shrugged. "Matt's another story, though, being a cop and all. Although I'm not sure how beholden to the badge he is at the moment, since he's on leave."

Kelly frowned. "On leave?"

"Yeah. It's not exactly a secret, I'm surprised he didn't say anything. Something about accumulated vacation time? Since he apparently worked some ridiculous hours after his divorce. Wait—did you know—?"

"Yes. Sabrina told me."

Abby nodded. "None of us liked Marcia very much. She was way too la-di-da for this family, that was for sure. But when things fell apart, so did Matt. Not in a dramatic way, I don't mean that—this is Matt we're talking about. But he kinda went all pod-person on us. Looked like Matt, sounded like Matt, but the real Matt wasn't home." She chuckled. "At work, yeah. But not at home. Anyway…if he didn't take his days, he was going to lose them. Or so he said. So he's around a lot, working on his house, bugging me. Big brothers are hell. You got any?"

Wow. Nothing like a little caffeine and carbs to ignite the jabberfest. "No, I'm an only child."

"Count your blessings. So were you and Matt close? When you were kids?"

"Not really, no." Even if not by Kelly's choice. A nugget of personal info she'd keep to herself. "He did his own thing, Sabrina and I did ours."

"Yeah, I can see that. Still, you should see Matt's place while you're here. He's put in some reclaimed stuff from the shop—the mantel is the bomb, from some nineteenth-century farmhouse."

Nope, not even penciling in that little field trip. Because, you know. Frying pans, fire, yada, yada.

Then two yawning children wandered into the kitchen, seeking hugs and nourishment. *This I can do,* Kelly thought as she set their filled bowls on the island and heaved her wild-haired daughter up onto a stool. And Abby immediately sucked Coop into a conversation, exactly as Jeanne would have done, and the ache in Kelly's chest eased a little more.

Because, for the moment, it was good to be back. To feel safe again.

Only then she thought of Matt. His eyes. His smile. His…everything. But especially his I-got-this attitude.

And that feeling-safe thing?

Gone.

Chapter Three

The instant Matt climbed out of his Explorer in the open-air lot near the Lincoln Tunnel, his face froze in the brutally cold wind. Between that and the five thousand bodies per square foot now swarming around him at roughly the speed of light, he remembered why he'd rather ice-skate naked than come into Manhattan. The crowds, the dirt, the noise… He flinched as a fire engine edging through the taxi-clogged street blasted its horn—so not him. And never would be.

Except since this was where his twin sister lived, this was where he needed to be. Because nobody understood how his brain worked better than Sabrina. Sure, they talked on the phone and texted, but their connection was strongest when they actually shared breathing space.

Made sense, he supposed, considering how, as suddenly orphaned six-year-olds, it'd been them against the world. Naturally Matt had felt honor bound to protect his sister, even though he later realized how much his scrappy little twin had protected him, too. And they were still there for each other, no matter what.

Bowed against the biting wind, he walked the few blocks to the Ninth Avenue diner where Sabrina had suggested they meet, one of those glaringly lit, grease-scented joints where the glasses were plastic, the plates weighed more than some of the patrons and fries came with, end of discussion.

Sabrina had snagged a booth near the back, looking like a slumming A-lister. Didn't act like one, though, squealing and bouncing up to throw her skinny, designer-clad arms around Matt.

"Sit, I already ordered for you," she said, immediately reverting to Jersey speak. "You look good. Worried, but good." Surrounded by a forest of artfully messy dark hair, equally dark, guilt-ridden eyes bored into his. "Damn. It's been too long, Matty."

"Hey. You're the one who spent the holidays out in Oyster Bay with your hotsy-totsy boyfriend."

"I know," she said with a mock pout. Which immediately turned into a huge grin…a moment before she thrust out her left hand, on which glittered a multistoned diamond ring that redefined *bling*.

"Well, look at that," Matt said, forcing his lips into a smile as a dozen conversations and clattering silverware and a ringing phone blurred around him. How could his sister marry someone he'd never even met? Still, he managed to say, "Congratulations," then stood and leaned over the table to kiss her cheek. "Lucky guy."

"Yes, he is," Bree said with an uncharacteristic giggle.

Just kill him now. "So when's the wedding?"

Their food arrived. Burgers and fries. Uninspired but comforting. "Not for at least a year. Plenty of time for you to get used to the idea." A grin flashed. "*And* Chad. Anyway…what's up? It must be something big to get you into the city."

Matt hoisted his hamburger off the plate, took a bite. His arteries were probably recoiling in terror, but his mouth was doing a happy dance. "When was the last time you talked to Kelly?"

Frowning, Sabrina grabbed her napkin to swipe dripping hamburger juice off her chin. "As in Kelly *McNeil?* I mean, Harrison, whatever."

"You know more than one?"

"No, but…" She put down the burger, wiped her hands, picked it up again. "Actually talked? Gosh… Ages ago. Since before she had her second kid. Why?"

"What's your take on her ex?"

Frowning, Sabrina swallowed, took a pull of her diet soda. "Okay, Matty? You can quit the whole detective shtick right now. What's going on?"

His sister was many things, but a faker wasn't one of them. Obviously she didn't know. "She and the kids are at the house."

Brows shot up. "You mean *our* house? Why? And why did I not know this?"

"Yeah, I'm getting to that, and she indicated you two had kind of drifted apart. Not to mention you changed your number."

"Crap, right. On both counts," she said with a disgusted-at-herself look, then squinted. "And you think Rick has something to do with her showing up?"

"Think, hell." His jaw tightened. "I know."

Sabrina's gaze sharpened. "And the man still has all his teeth?"

"What—?"

"Oh, come on, Matty—it's not like nobody knew how

you felt about her back in the day. Although I couldn't figure out why you never acted on it—"

"Why *I* never acted on it?" His sister smiled, and he realized he'd walked right into her trap. "So maybe I felt something for her. Since she didn't exactly give me any encouragement, I didn't pursue it."

"Idiot."

"Excuse me?"

"You really never noticed how Kelly clammed up whenever you came into the room?"

"Sure I noticed. Figured that was her way of telling me not to bother—"

"You can't be serious! She was crazy for you! But you'd waltz in, all swagger and strut like the world was yours, and she'd think, 'What chance would I have with *him?*'"

"She actually told you that?"

Bree made the Scout's honor sign.

Matt gaped at his sister for several seconds before he found his voice. "Why didn't you say anything?"

"Because, for one thing, you did act like you were all that back then. I'm not even sure *I* liked you very much, to be truthful. So I sure as hell wasn't inclined to fix you up with my best friend. Even if you did have a thing for her." She jabbed a fry in his direction. "Which I'm guessing you still do. Since you're here and all."

"I'm *here* because Kelly is about to violate her custody agreement, if she hasn't already, and I figured if anyone could shed some light on why she's doing that, it'd be you."

Sabrina finished her burger, then wiped her fingers on her already crumpled napkin. "You don't believe whatever she's told you?"

His gut twisted. "I don't know her, Bree. You do. Or did, anyway."

"And if I put your mind at ease? *Then* will you go smack him around?"

Matt almost smiled. "It's not like I can go vigilante on the guy's ass. Since, oddly enough, I would like to have a job to go back to. And—" he leaned forward "—this is strictly between us, okay? Even if her story pans out, I'm still really pushing it by letting her stay at the house."

"Jeez, you make it sound like she offed the guy." Her brow furrowed. "Do we know that she didn't?" she said, and Matt smiled again. They'd both thought the same thing.

"I heard her talking to him this morning, so yeah. He's still alive."

"He said, gritting his teeth."

Matt glowered at his sister. Who, of course, laughed at him. "Bree…get real. What I felt—that was a long time ago, when none of us had a clue about, well, anything really. And after Marcia… Hell, I don't want to even look at that horse, let alone get back up on it." And his sister didn't know the half of it. Neither did anyone else. "And no," he said to Bree's lifted brows, "I'm not calling Marcia a horse. Anyway, I'm not entirely sure what's going on, I didn't hear much of the conversation, but last night Kelly seemed pretty convinced that Rick might hurt the children."

"Holy crap—are you serious?"

"She certainly is. And if what she's telling me is legit…" He sighed. "You know how I feel about this stuff. I'm not gonna let anything happen to her or the kids, if I can help it. But you can see my dilemma."

"Yeah," Bree sighed out, then caught their waitress's eye and ordered a piece of cherry pie. "Okay," she said after the pie arrived, "for what it's worth, I only met Rick twice, and once was at their wedding when he was on his best behavior. Although even then, alarms went off. The second time was right after Cooper was born. Which is when I decided my initial suspicions had been dead-on."

"Meaning?"

"He was—is?—full of himself, for one thing. Controlling as hell, for another. Not that I dared say anything, Kelly was clearly head over heels with the guy. And obviously okay with letting him rule the roost."

Bree speared a hunk of the pie, pointed it at him. "What I said earlier? About how you intimidated her when we were kids? That wasn't only because you were being a butt, but because Kelly wasn't exactly the most secure *chica* in Jersey. Her parents… I swear, she couldn't go pee without their permission. Frankly, I think the only reason they let her come over was because they figured—rightly—there'd be no funny stuff with Dad around."

She finally pushed the bite into her mouth. "Anyway… even if watching Rick and Kelly together gave me the willies, I figured as long as Kell was happy, what business was it of mine? But then Rick lost his job, and, well… I worried then how that would impact their—" she pressed her lips together for a moment "—balance. Because I got the feeling, even from reading between the lines when she wrote, that she finally started to find her footing the same time he lost his. And that he didn't take it well."

"Score one for you," Matt said, and Bree made a tick mark in the air. "Kelly ever say Rick…hurt her?"

"Physically? No. But I could definitely tell Kelly wasn't happy. So, frankly, I was relieved when she admitted she'd asked for a divorce. I also know how much it must have wrecked her."

"So she said. She also indicated things got worse with Rick after that."

Bree sighed. "That would not surprise me. But here's the

thing about Kelly. Two things, actually. One, she's fiercely loyal. Even in school she was never fickle with her friendships, like so many other girls were. Which was why it was so hard for her to split from Rick. And why, maybe, she might not be telling you, or even being totally honest with herself, about how bad things were between them. I mean, who knows, right? But she's also law-abiding to a fault—no going over the speed limit, no crossing against the light. Made me nuts when we were younger, until I realized that, for her, obedience equated security." She twisted to dig her phone out of her purse beside her on the seat. "So if she is violating that agreement, she must have a really good reason. Honey, believe me—you're never gonna find anyone more trustworthy, I swear." Glancing over as she rummaged, she said, "That help?"

"Yes. And no."

"I know, sweetie," Bree said gently, reaching over to squeeze Matt's wrist before, her phone retrieved, she flicked her hair over her shoulder, then scrolled through her contacts. "Did she give you her cell number?"

"Yeah," he said, pulling out his own phone and reading it off.

"That's the one I have. I'll call her tonight. But you be sure she has my number, too." Then she stood and dropped her phone back in her purse. "And unfortunately, I've got an appointment downtown in twenty minutes—"

Matt grabbed the check. "You go, I've got it."

"You sure?"

"For God's sake, Bree—"

Laughing, she hugged him, then scooted through the lunchtime crowd, leaving him with that bittersweet feeling he got every time they parted that she didn't need him anymore. Hadn't, actually, in a very long time.

Outside the wind had died down, giving the feeble winter sunshine half a shot at warming the poor slobs hustling through the concrete canyons. Hands plowed into the pockets of his Giants jacket, Matt slowed his pace, halfheartedly glancing in store windows as he meandered back to his car. Normally he'd be champing at the bit to blow this town, get back home. Except currently that meant returning to something he was less sure how to handle now than he had been this morning.

And it was driving him crazy that he wasn't becoming *more* sure-footed as he got older.

His entire adult life, he'd relied on his instincts to guide him. On the traits that made him who he was, that had propelled him into law enforcement without a second thought. Traits he'd assumed would make him a good husband. A good man. For someone who'd only ever wanted to do the right thing—at least, once out of the clutches of adolescence—it had come as a shock to discover that not everyone defined *right,* or even *good,* the same way.

Like, say, his ex-wife.

Oh, in theory he understood why his marriage fell apart. God knows Marcia had told him often enough, and plainly enough, that his breathing down her neck with wanting to take care of her made her crazy. But Matt's only motive had been to make sure she was safe, that her brakes were good and her tires inflated, that she locked all the doors when he had to work late, that she didn't take unnecessary risks when *she* was out late.

Just like his father had done for his mother. Who, as far as Matt could tell, had never had an issue with being taken care of. Watched out for. A good example, he'd thought. Only, according to his ex, his attitude was out-of-date, paternalistic and condescending.

He still didn't get that.

Speaking of his dad, who needed to know he had a

houseguest… Matt pulled his phone out of his inside pocket, took a breath and dialed.

"Matt!" his father boomed in his ear. "What's up?"

Even at nearly seventy, Preston Noble still sounded like a man half his age. But with an aura of omniscience—not to mention omnipotence—that had kept all of them in line as kids. And his father still commanded both deference and respect, Matt thought on a wry smile. He loved his old man, was more grateful than he could say that he and Jeanne had taken Sabrina and him into their home, their hearts. But it wasn't always easy living up to the Colonel's expectations. Or sometimes even knowing what those expectations were.

Along with a dozen fellow pedestrians, he stopped at a side street to let a line of honking cars wade through the bumpy intersection. "How's Uncle Phil and Aunt Vickie?"

"Fine. And something tells me you didn't call to ask about them."

A thousand miles away and he still didn't miss a trick. "Okay, I'm not." He squinted into the traffic. "You remember Kelly McNeil?"

"Considering she basically lived at our house for ten years? Of course." A truck driver blasted his horn at some woman on her phone who'd darted out in front of him. "Where are you?"

"In the city," Matt shouted over the din. "Came in to see Bree. Anyway… Kelly. She's at the house. With her kids."

"She is? How come?"

The light changed. Matt fell in step with the herd surging across the street, filling in his dad as he walked. When he finished, his father released a breath.

"And you're going to help her."

An order, not a question. Now it was Matt's turn to

sigh, his breath frosting around his mouth. "Not sure what I can do—"

"Your mother loved that girl, you know. Or maybe you don't. Of course, Jeannie would have taken in every needy kid in the world, if she could have," Preston said on a slight laugh. "But that one had a special place in her heart. She said Kelly always seemed so…fragile. Like she'd break if you looked at her funny."

Before Matt could interject, his father continued. "Her parents' fault, if you ask me. They were good people, don't get me wrong. And your mother and I liked them well enough. But there's a fine line between protecting your kids and smothering them. And they crossed it."

"Huh. Sabrina said pretty much the same thing."

"We could never figure out how the girl could hang around your sister—hell, any of you kids—and not have some of that spunk rub off on her. But it didn't. At least not before her father died, and her mother and she moved away." He paused. "How's she doing?"

"Hard to tell. Although I think she found that spunk. At least enough to get herself and her kids out of what sounds like a bad situation."

"Spunk, hell. That takes *guts.* Which you know."

His father was only echoing what Matt had said to Kelly that morning. Words Matt had meant with every fiber of his being. So why did he feel like rats were gnawing at him from the inside out?

"So you're okay, then," he said, "with her being here?"

"Why wouldn't I be? Can't tell you how often your mother mentioned Kelly after they moved. Asked Sabrina if she'd heard from her, how she was making out. And I know for a fact if Jeannie were still here, she'd be gratified that Kelly felt she could come to us. So you take good care of her. And as it happens…I was going to call tonight, anyway. Think I might stay down here a little longer."

"Really? How much longer?"

"Haven't decided." Pop laughed. "Although the way the weather's been up there, I may not come back until June. I didn't figure you'd mind."

"Um, no, of course not—"

"Abby okay? The other boys?"

The "boys" being Matt's adopted brothers. Tyler, the youngest, was always "okay," as far as Matt could tell, his salvage business growing like gangbusters as he went through girlfriends like popcorn. Matt's older brother, Ethan, however, was another case entirely, parenting four kids on his own after his wife's death three years earlier.

But they were all adults now, making their own choices and decisions. After raising them, not to mention everything their father had gone through during their mother's illness, the old man deserved to live his own life. Have a little fun. Soak up the Florida sunshine. So Matt reassured the Colonel they were all good, to go frolic with the gators as long as he liked.

The call finished, and it occurred to Matt that, actually, the whole making-your-own-choices thing was a crock. Or at least a myth. Especially when fate had other ideas.

Because if it were up to *him,* he thought, stopping in front of a toy-store window, he'd still be married. Maybe a dad himself by now. If it were up to *him*—he went inside, just to look—redheaded crushes from his past would have stayed in his past, not shown up in his present to seriously mess with his head. If it were up to *him*—he picked up a *Star Wars* LEGO set, put it back, picked it up again—his sister would have given him every reason to boot said redhead back to Haleysburg to work out her problems with her ex. And his father wouldn't have twisted the knife by playing the your-mother-would-have-wanted-this card.

The mother who'd saved his sorry butt when he'd been too little to know his butt needing saving.

Never mind the risk involved, he thought as he plunked the LEGO set, as well as a brightly colored sock monkey, on the counter by the cash register and pulled out his wallet, should he *get* involved.

His phone buzzed as the cashier handed him back his credit card, the bagged toys. *And not only to your career, bonehead,* he thought when he saw Kelly's name and number in the display, and his heart thumped.

"Hey…what's up?" he said, aiming for casual…which went right out the window when he heard Kelly's next-door-to-hysterical laugh in his ear. No, not a laugh, some sound that defied description. Now outside, his hand tightened around the phone. "Kelly—?"

"Rick's dead," she choked out, then burst into sobs.

Chapter Four

It wasn't until the front door opened that Kelly realized she hadn't moved from the floor in front of the family room sofa for more than an hour. The dog sashayed out, only to return a moment later with Matt, who immediately kneeled in front of her, his gaze focused. Kind, yes, but all business. Thank God.

"Where's the kids?" he asked.

"With your sister. She'd offered to take them to Target while I went over to the kitchen. My catering kitchen, I mean. I've got a job this weekend...." Bile rose in her throat. She shut her eyes, willing the world to stop spinning. Matt wrapped his hand around hers. She didn't object. Couldn't.

"What happened?" he asked gently, and her stomach twisted. A hundred times, she'd probably replayed Lynn's words in her head, but she hadn't yet said them out loud.

"Best guess is a heart attack," Kelly whispered, keeping her eyes averted. Afraid to look at Matt, knowing she'd fall apart if she did. Even more afraid to acknowledge the vicious, nonstop voices inside her head that it was her fault, that she'd given up and walked away and now he was dead and *it was her fault, her fault, her fault....* "But no one knows for sure. His m-mother found him in his room. The poor woman...."

Her eyes flooded again as sadness swamped her. Letting go of her hand, Matt grabbed a box of tissues from the end table, held it out. Kelly yanked one from the box and pressed it to her mouth until she could speak.

"Rick was Lynn's only child. She was already heartsick. I can't imagine what she's going through. I should be with her, but I couldn't leave until—"

The garage door rumbled open. Kelly's eyes shot to Matt's as her heart bounded into her throat. He'd gone perfectly still, his breathing calm and steady, like Rick's had been in the delivery room with Coop, back when things were good. When she'd taken "forever" for granted, could have never imagined what would happen. But now it was Matt holding her gaze, being a rock in the midst of her turbulent emotions, helping her breathe through a pain she doubted anyone else would understand. And for the moment—since this is all it was, this freakish, momentary intersection of their lives—she was grateful.

She struggled to her feet. "I should get the kids' things together."

"Why?" Matt said, standing, as well.

"Um, so we can go back home? Since we don't need to hide out anymore?"

"Plenty of time to do that tomorrow. Or whenever." At her undoubtedly puzzled expression, he said, "Don't you think it might be better to let the kids stay in a neutral zone for now? Especially Cooper."

Cooper. Oh, dear God. Fresh tears sprang to her eyes.

"How am I going to t-tell him, Matt?" At his frown, she said, "It wasn't all bad. I swear. Not for a long time, at least. Coop used to *worship* his daddy. And I think what hurts the most is that, in spite of everything, he probably still does. Or at least wants to."

For a moment, something sharp flickered through Matt's eyes. Then his gaze softened. "Do you want me to tell him?"

Not in a million years was that going to happen. Even so, catching her haggard reflection in a nearby mirror, she sighed. But then, why shouldn't she be upset? Whatever had happened between her and Rick, this was a horrible shock. Was going to be horrible for some time. And to pretend otherwise would be hideously unfair to their son.

"Thanks. But no."

"You sure?"

Not at all. But such was life, right? Nodding, Kelly turned back to Matt. Concern buckled his forehead and her heart swelled. For his goodness, if nothing else. That he'd grown up even better than she'd imagined he would.

Whereas she was still a very shaky work in progress.

"I've spent far too much of my life avoiding the hard stuff, letting other people run interference for me. The last thing I need to do right now is let Cooper think his mother is a wuss."

"He will never think that," Matt said softly, a moment before Abby and the children burst into the room. Coop took one look at her and stopped dead in his tracks.

"Mom? What's wrong?"

Not even bothering to check her tears, Kelly opened her arms.

"What're you doing out here?"

Slouched in one of the big rattan chairs in the sunroom

off the dining room, Matt shrugged at Abby's question. "Thinking," he said, stretching out one foot to lay it on the matching ottoman.

"That's not like you," she said, and he smiled in spite of the knot in his chest. "You okay?"

"Me being okay isn't the issue."

Abby tromped across the terra-cotta-tiled floor and dropped into another chair a few feet away. "Which is why I don't get why you're out here and not in there."

"Did you see the look Cooper gave me after Kelly told him about his dad?"

"Please don't tell me you think that was really aimed at you? For God's sake, the kid was in shock."

Punching out a frustrated breath, Matt pressed his thumb and forefinger against his eyelids, still trying to figure out how the world could go ass-over-teakettle in less than a day. Bad enough that some chick he'd never expected to see again shows up out of the blue, but then her ex—who was the reason for her showing up to begin with—*dies?* Holy hell. Although you'd think, considering how often life had clobbered him in the past, he'd be used to it by now. Coop, however…

Matt squinted against the glare of late-day sunlight slashing across the leftover snow outside. No, he didn't know the kid. Or, beyond what Kelly had told him, anything about his relationship with his father. But he understood the upheaval and uncertainty, the "what comes next?" the kid was probably feeling. And Abby was right, the boy's reaction wasn't personal. In fact, it had nothing to do with Matt. A fact that would probably make a lot of men sigh in relief.

Except *relieved* was one thing he most definitely was not right now, logic be damned. Frustrated as hell was more like it—

"You're pissed that you can't fix this, aren't you?" Abby said, startling him.

"What?"

A slight, slightly smart-ass smile touched his sister's mouth before she stood, contorting her arms into the most painful-looking position to crack her spine. Then, releasing what sounded like a blissful sigh, Abby punched her hands into her hoodie pockets. "I know that look. God knows I've seen it often enough. And not just on your face. On Dad's, too. Never mind that you haven't seen this woman in years, that you don't know these kids. If someone's in trouble, you want to make it better. No...you *have* to. Am I right?"

Glaring at the backyard, Matt locked his hands behind his head. "Yeah. And maybe that's why I do what I do."

"And we all love you for it," his sister said, leaning over to give him a quick hug. "Most of the time, anyway."

Matt pushed out a dry chuckle and Abby straightened, her hands in her pockets again. And maybe it was the light, or because his brain was on overload, but suddenly he saw a...seriousness behind the sparkle in those bright blue eyes he'd never noticed before. Huh. His baby sister was all grown up.

Then her gaze shifted to the open French doors behind him. Matt twisted around, surging to his feet when he saw Kelly in her coat and scarf, her curls abandoned to fend for themselves. In the stark light she looked paler than ever, her hand tightly fisted around the purse strap straddling her shoulder.

"I hate to ask, but..." A nervous smile flickered around her mouth, apology screaming behind those ridiculous glasses. "I really do need to go see Rick's mom for a little while, but...I'm not sure I should take the kids—"

"I'm so sorry," Abby said. "I'd be glad to watch them, but I've got to get back to work—"

"You go on, Abs," Matt said. "I'll stay."

"You're sure?" Kelly said as Abby hustled past her. "I mean, if it's a problem I'll take them—"

"Kelly, for crying out loud, I ride herd with Ethan's rugrats all the time. I've got this, okay?"

"Except these rugrats just lost their father. I mean, Aislin's okay—about that, anyway, she doesn't really understand what's going on, although God forbid you give her the wrong sippy cup, your ears will never be the same. But Coop…" Her chin trembled for a moment, killing Matt. She looked back—no, more like leaned back—into the house. "He didn't say a single word when I told him. Didn't cry, nothing." Worried eyes met his again. "Is that even normal?"

Given what she'd said? The kid's emotions were probably more tangled than Kelly's hair. "Everyone reacts differently—"

"I shouldn't leave him, should I? I mean, I know Lynn needs me, too, she doesn't have anyone else, but she is an adult. *Damn* it—" Kelly shoved the heel of her hand into her temple. "Why can't I figure out what to *do?*"

Speaking of tangled emotions…. "It's okay," Matt said, wanting to hold her. Wanting to run. Most of all, to wind back the clock. "Really. We'll all get through this, I promise."

After a moment, she nodded, clutching that purse strap like she'd fall into the abyss if she let go. "I should be back by dinnertime. I hope. And they're in the family room, watching a movie—"

At that, Matt took her by the shoulders, gently swiveling her toward the front door. "You can call me every five minutes if it'll ease your mind. But the sooner you go, the sooner you'll be back."

Her eyes searched his for a moment before, with another nod, she left.

In the family room, Aislin lay on the carpet, staring blankly up at the beamed ceiling, thumb in mouth. Matt figured the toddler had five minutes, tops, before she zonked out. Coop, however, was scrunched up next to Alf in the sectional's corner, head propped in hand, gaze fixed at the garishly hued figures cavorting across the fifty-inch screen.

"Hey," Matt said softly. Alf thumped her tail, but neither kid responded. Matt entered the room, the seen-better-days recliner wobbling and groaning when he sat on its edge.

"You don't have to stay," Coop said, not looking at Matt. "I'm watching Linnie."

"I can see that." Matt leaned forward, his hands clasped together. "Just checking in."

God knew he'd been around enough kids that they didn't scare him, like they did some men. Actually, he thought they were pretty awesome, the way they processed the world around them, how they'd say whatever popped into their brains. Ethan's brood slayed him, the stuff that came out of their mouths. Of course, some kids were harder to read, to connect with. Same as adults. But Matt discovered some time ago he liked the challenge, figuring out how to make that connection. Like the Colonel used to do. Yeah, he'd studied under the master, for sure.

"Whatcha watching?"

Coop gave the tiniest shoulder shrug and said, "I'm not. But movies help Linnie fall asleep, so Mom put it on."

Matt nodded, then asked, "You okay?"

The boy reached up to rub his eye underneath his glasses, knocking them askew. Shoving them back into place, he shrugged again.

"Hungry?"

Alf lifted her bearlike head, ears perked, her tail thumping with a little more oomph. Dogs were supposed to understand about one hundred and fifty words, Matt had heard. In Alf's case, at least ninety percent of those were food related.

"No. Thanks."

The beast swiveled her massive head toward the boy, before, with an equally massive doggy sigh, lowering her chin back onto her front paws. From a few feet away, Matt caught the slow-motion drift to earth of Aislin's hand as her thumb disconnected from her sagged-open mouth. He pushed himself up to grab the afghan from the back of the sectional, crouching to carefully drape it over the now-sleeping baby.

"Mom does that, too," Coop said behind him, and Matt glanced over his shoulder. His forehead slightly knotted, the boy was looking at his sister. "Lets her sleep wherever. Because she'll wake up if you try to move her."

Stretching out his back muscles as he rose, Matt smiled. "Abby was like that, too. So I know the drill."

"Abby said you took care of her a lot when she was little."

"We all did. All of us kids, I mean. She was like another pet. But louder. And smellier."

Coop sort of smiled. "Mom said Linnie doesn't know. That Dad died."

Matt sat again on the recliner. "She's a little young, yeah."

"So she won't even remember him?"

Sad though the conversation was, that the boy was even talking to him warmed Matt through. It took a lot to earn a child's trust. As well he knew. "Maybe not. I sure don't remember anything from when I was three. Do you?"

The boy's forehead scrunched harder. Then he shook his

head. "Not really." He shifted on the sofa; the dog shifted right with him. Then they all fell into a silence so brittle Matt could practically feel the air molecules shattering between them. A silence brought on, he suspected, by a little boy's holding in a boatload of thoughts and feelings that would only keep multiplying and expanding until they nearly strangled him. He knew that drill, too.

"Um…if you want to keep talking, I'm a pretty good listener."

This time, Coop shot him an are-you-nuts glance, then faced the TV again. "Why would I do that?"

"Because sometimes it helps. To get all the stuff crammed in your head *out* of your head—"

"That's okay, thanks."

"Just an idea," he said with a doesn't-matter-to-me hitch of his shoulders. "Anyway, you'd probably rather talk to your mom—"

The child's emphatic head shake both confirmed Matt's suspicions and told him not to push. Not the time or the place. Or his place, frankly.

"Well, okay, then." Matt plucked a paperback novel he was halfway through off the coffee table. "If you need me, I'm right in the living room. Okay?"

"Sure," the kid said, pointing the remote at the screen to switch back to cable, clearly not caring one whit whether Matt stayed or went.

Kelly didn't get back to Maple River until nearly eight, at which point all she wanted to do was fall into bed, any bed, and not wake up for three days. But alas, there were children who needed to be tucked in and cuddled with and, in Coop's case, reassured, and after all that she was somewhat reenergized. *Somewhat* being the operative word.

And hungry, she realized, since she hadn't eaten since

breakfast, despite Lynn's food-pushing attempts. So when she entered the kitchen and Matt greeted her with a sandwich big enough to feed the Bronx, she almost kissed him. Which only proved how exhausted she was.

"Kids asleep?" he asked.

"Finally, yes. Alfie's in bed with Coop. I hope that's okay?"

"You kidding? She's in heaven. Although fair warning, she snores. And the kid'll smell like dog in the morning."

"He's smelled worse, believe me."

Finally she hauled herself up onto the bar stool, only to then rest her head in her hands for a moment.

"Praying?" Matt asked.

"Yes. For the strength to eat this." Kelly lifted her head to see the sorta smile peeking out from that whiskered face, thinking how strong he looked. And how weak she felt. In more ways than one. She didn't want hanky-panky—she was far too tired and emotionally drained for hanky-panky—but once again the thought niggled that it might be nice to be held by someone bigger than she was. And blessed with a Y chromosome. "And what's this?" she asked when he placed a tall glass in front of her.

"A chocolate shake. With extra protein. Another of my specialties. And yes, you need to drink it—the skeletal look is not good on you."

Tears seared her eyes because she was about to keel over and her world was still imploding and she had so much on her plate that stuff was spilling over the sides, and this man had made her a chocolate milk shake. With extra protein.

"Hey," Matt said quietly, when she realized she'd made this pathetic little hiccupping sound. She looked up into those lovely brown eyes all soft with concern. And hiccupped again. "It's okay, the kids are okay, you're here and we've got it covered."

"We?"

"Me. Abby. The dog. So eat. Then take a hot bath and go to bed. How's that sound?"

"Like heaven." Kelly took a deep breath, then bit into the sandwich. And groaned. "Oh, my God—what's in this?"

"Whatever I could scrounge up. Beef. Turkey. Bacon. Salad stuff. And some Asian dressing I found in the door, I assume belonging to my sister."

"Speaking of heaven…" She pointed to the sandwich. "Dude."

Matt grinned. One of those grins that, had she not been so tired, had life not been so insane, had this not been her and Matt…

Eat your sandwich, chickie.

"How were the kids?" she said, tilting the shake to her lips.

"Fine. Baby passed out ten minutes after you left, ate a huge bowl of mac and cheese when she woke up, after which she terrorized the dog until right before you got back."

"I'm so sorry—"

"Forget it, Alf needed the exercise, anyway. You weren't kidding about my ears, though. Wow. Kid's got a wicked set of lungs. I'm thinking opera singer."

"You're not the first person to put forth that idea. And Coop?"

Matt leaned his jeaned butt against the edge of the counter, crossing his arms. "Pretty tight-lipped. Then again, he doesn't know me from Adam."

Her brows knotting, Kelly pinched off a little tongue of bacon taunting her from the edge of the bread, poked it into her mouth. "I know you and Bree were only six when your folks died, but…do you remember at all how it felt?"

His eyes dimmed. “Some. And I wasn’t exactly chatty, either. So. I assume there’s a funeral?”

And you’re still not talking about it, are you?

Kelly took another sip of her shake. “On Friday, yes. The, um, autopsy should be done by then,” she said, knowing the icy feeling in her chest had nothing to do with the shake. “But the consensus is that it really was a heart attack. Probably related to his drinking.”

“How’s Rick’s mom holding up?”

Note, he hadn’t asked how *she* was doing. Not that she really wanted him to. Kindness was one thing—that, she was soaking up like soft butter on hot toast—but pity? Not a fan. Especially since “holding it together by the tips of my ragged fingernails” would have been the answer. But with two kids depending on her, what choice did she have?

“Keeping herself busy,” she finally answered. “Like my mother did after my dad died. Lynn’s already taken care of the arrangements, everything. It’ll hit, though, I’m sure. And I really should be there for her. After the funeral, I mean. She’s always been a sweetheart, no matter what. I owe her a lot. Except…”

She dispatched the last bite of the sandwich’s first half, picked up the second. “Since I was in town, anyway, I stopped by our apartment to pick up some more clothes. And the minute I walked in, I realized how much I do not want to stay in Haleysburg. Not because it’s a horrible place or anything, but it’s never been…home. A convenience, a concession, yes. But it never felt right. Especially when Coop started having so much trouble in school—”

“Trouble? What kind of trouble?”

“Teasing, mostly. Because of his weight. His glasses. Added to his father’s taunting him…” She half shrugged. “It was bad.”

“I assume you talked to the principal?”

"Until I was blue in the face. Nothing happened. Then, last fall, some kid twice Coop's size shoved him down on the playground, broke his glasses and that was it. I yanked him out of there so fast we left a vapor trail."

"Shazam," Matt said, and Kelly smiled. "So were things better at his new school?"

"Actually, we've been homeschooling." At Matt's slight brow dip, she said, "The kid was getting stomachaches every day, Matt. Even with everything else going on, those stopped almost immediately. And after a couple months I realized his weight had started to normalize, too."

Kelly picked up the cold glass, gently swirling the melting shake. "Sometimes the best decision isn't the one that makes the most sense on the surface. Like taking your kid out of school to homeschool him," she said with a shrug. "And now, well… I didn't realize how much I'd missed Maple River until Bree called me a couple hours ago." At Matt's almost imperceptible flinch, she softly laughed. "Yeah, she told me about the grilling. It's okay—in your place I would've done the same thing."

"I didn't tell her to call you, though."

"I know you didn't. But in any case, I heard her voice, and…" Smiling, she shook her head, then sighed. "I want to move back. Have the kids grow up where I did."

"You serious?"

There was something in his voice, his expression, she couldn't read. Horror, most likely. After all, it wasn't as if Maple River had anything special going for it. One small Jersey town was pretty much like any other. And heaven knows Sabrina couldn't wait to blow the joint. Then again, since the Colonel's other kids still lived here, how bad could it be?

"Now that things…have changed, there's really nothing stopping me. The lease is up this month on my catering kitchen, so I'll have to find a new one, anyway. Apartment prices are a little steeper here than in Haleysburg, but there are a couple possibilities that don't look too bad. And Lynn's only a half hour away. So totally doable."

Matt kept her gaze on his for a long moment, then removed her empty plate—the same blue-and-white-patterned Corelle Kelly remembered from before. "Abby made cookies after work," he said, setting the plate in the dishwasher. "Want some?"

"You think I'm crazy."

He turned. "*Crazy* might be a little strong. Impulsive, maybe? Not that it's any of my business—"

"No. It isn't. Not that I don't appreciate the concern. No, I really do. But the longer I think about it, the more I realize this has been simmering in the back of my mind for, gosh, I don't know how long, buried underneath a pile of obligations and responsibilities that kept me paralyzed. And I'm not an idiot, I know this has a lot to do with memories of my childhood. Of my time in this house, with you guys. When I felt happy. And safe. So sue me if I'd like to try to recapture some of that for my babies. To give them a fresh start." She sat back. "To give myself a fresh start. And why are you smiling?"

"Because the whole time you were telling me off, all I could think was, *damn*."

"I wasn't telling you off—"

"Like hell. And you can stay here as long as you want. Okay?"

"Oh. I didn't mean to—"

"Okay?"

Kelly almost smiled. "Okay. Thank you."

"No problem. Now. You want some cookies or what?"

"You are so weird."

"So I've been told. So…?"

She blew out a breath. "No, thanks. Not much feeling like sweets right now."

Matt shook his head, then said, "Coffee, then? Decaf?"

"That I'll go for. Where is Abby, by the way?"

He got the coffee out of the fridge, went about filling the basket. "*Now* you ask this?"

"I'm awake now. Anyway. Abby?"

"She's out. With a friend. A *girl* friend," he said at Kelly's lifted brow. "She doesn't date. Says it's not her thing." His hands lifted. "I don't ask."

With her fingertip, Kelly swiped a dribble of dressing off the plate, sucking her finger for a moment before saying, "You mind if I ask *you* something?"

"About?"

"Abby said you're on leave from work? Because you'd accumulated so many vacation days?"

"Ah." He got out two mugs, filled them. Set one in front of her with a carton of half-and-half, a divided bowl with sugar on one side, assorted wannabes on the other. Clearly stalling.

"Hey, if you don't want to talk about it—"

"It's no big deal, despite whatever Abs might've told you. It's just after my divorce, I had a lot of time on my hands. So I worked. A lot. Filled in whenever someone went on vacation, that sort of thing. Eventually my sergeant caught on and put me on leave." He met her gaze, almost as though daring her to probe further. "Which at least is forcing me to finish up the house."

Kelly took a sip of her coffee, opting not to press him about an obviously still painful subject. "Abby mentioned that, too. Close by?"

"Five blocks east...." Matt frowned down at his coffee for several seconds before his eyes met hers again, his Adam's apple bobbing. "There's a basement apartment.

Not huge, but three bedrooms and the kitchen's not total crap—" She laughed, and a grin flashed. "Anyway. You could see it. If you want, it's up to you. Yard's big, schools are good I hear. If you decide to go that route, I mean. And Alf would be thrilled to have her own boy. But like I said, it's up to you, no pressure."

Kelly tapped the mug's rim, considering. "Why?"

"You need an apartment. I have one."

He was such a guy. She smiled. "How much?"

Matt named his price. Two hundred dollars a month less than she'd been paying in Haleysburg. For three bedrooms and good schools—and yes, they were, she'd already checked, even though she wasn't sure about putting Coop in another classroom setting right now—and a yard and a bonus dog.

And Matt, of course. But she was a big girl—for good schools and a yard she could handle Matt. Or rather, not handle Matt.

"Could we see it tomorrow?"

"Uh…sure. Why not? And by the way—" he stood up straighter "—I'm coming with you to the funeral. Because, for starters," he said when her chin dropped, "I can hear my mother telling me to keep an eye on you. Not to mention my dad."

So could she, actually, but that was beside the point. "I don't need—"

"And for another, that's what friends do."

Those brown eyes captured hers.

And. Would. Not. Let. Go.

"Is that what we are? Friends?"

His shoulders bumped. "Sure."

Then she got it. This wasn't about his mother, or their being friends—which was a stretch, anyway. Really. This was about Matt thinking he had to protect her. Which was sweet and honorable and all that, but…

Uh, boy.

"Okay, look—I know I was a mess earlier. After I found out, I mean. But that… It was a momentary reaction. I'm fine now."

He crossed his arms. Man speak for *not buying it, sister.* "You sure?"

"Yes. I was shocked. Obviously. But—" Kelly shoved a hunk of hair behind her ear "—I really did mourn the death of my marriage. But the thing is, Rick and I… We'd *both* changed. God knows even five years ago I would have never believed I could fall out of love with my husband. Only, who I'd fallen in love with…that man no longer existed. Okay, I supposed I'd clung to this *tiny* hope that Rick would find the real Rick again, someone the kids and I could at least respect. But that didn't happen."

She sighed. "And now it'll never happen, which makes me sad. And I'll probably always be sad about that to a certain extent, because I had loved him and I certainly never wanted things to end so…hopelessly. So in a way, I am grieving again. For the past, for what might have been. But trust me—I'm not going to fall apart at this funeral." After a pause, she said, "If I've learned nothing else about myself these past two years, it's that I'm stronger, and smarter, and a helluva lot more resilient than I thought I was. That I can take care of myself. And my children."

One hand clamped around the edge of the granite, Matt hooked her gaze in his. "I don't doubt that for a second. But you're gonna have your hands full with your kids. Your mother-in-law. So it might not hurt to have someone there for *you* who isn't emotionally involved. To run interference, if necessary. Still. Your call. You really don't want me to come, I won't."

And, oh, she really didn't. Except now that the turkey had put the idea in her head, she kinda did. Just for backup. Like an angel presence.

A six-foot-two, beard-hazed, smart-mouthed angel with overachieving biceps. God had outdone Himself with this one.

"The old ladies will have you for lunch."

"Wouldn't be a Jersey funeral otherwise," Matt said with a whatcha-gonna-do shrug, and Kelly rolled her eyes.

The house's main utilities once more in working order, Matt had taken a good, hard look at the basement apartment's kitchen and thought, *This will never do.* Never mind that Kelly had been fine with it as it was. Nor was he gonna go all out or anything, especially since the rent he'd quoted was under market value. *Well* under market value. Which she undoubtedly knew. Smart cookie, that Kelly. But while the kitchen did function, the cabinets were from hunger and the appliances had been old twenty years ago. So what the hell, a little upgrade couldn't hurt, right?

"I cannot believe Kelly McNeil is moving in here," his youngest brother, Tyler, said as he drilled one of the "new" cabinets into the wall while Matt supported it. White Shaker style, barely two years old, victims of a total gut-job in Princeton. Although at least their previous owner had the decency to put them up for adoption at Ty's salvage shop, where Matt got them for a song. Ty reached for another screw. "Talk about a blast from the past."

"And I can't believe you remember her."

Underneath a mop of streaked blond hair, super-straight teeth flashed in a clean-shaven face. Thirty going on eighteen, that was his brother.

"You kidding?" Ty pressed a hand to his hoodie-covered chest. "She was my first love."

"You were nine, for God's sake."

"And Mozart was how old when he composed his first symphony?"

Matt groaned, but he had to laugh, too. Ty had been an insolent, foul-mouthed fourth-grader when he'd come to live with the Nobles, a real pain in the butt as far as thirteen-year-old Matt had been concerned. Nor had he understood why on earth his parents adopted the brat a year after that, especially since his mother had her hands full by then with toddler Abby.

Only later did Matt discover that Ty's birth mother had been a druggie, that he'd been removed from her care for his own safety. And that CPS had all but begged his parents to foster him, hoping the neglected kid might find comfort and stability in his parents' orderly household. Which, eventually, he did. And aside from his brother's inability to sustain a relationship for more than a month, the goofball had turned out okay.

"So where is Kelly now?" Ty said, interrupting Matt's thoughts. In a parallelogram of sunlight slashed across the living room floor, a dead-to-the-world Alf released one of her foghorn groans, making Boomer, Ty's hideously homely boxer/Rottweiler mix, jump to his feet with a very confused look on his droopy face, and Matt smiled.

"Back in Haleysburg," he said, "packing. She wants to move in right after the funeral, so we need to hustle. By the way…I found your old Power Rangers bike in Dad's garage. Looks to be in decent shape, aside from the tires and tubes. I thought I might fix it up, give it to Cooper. If you don't want it…?"

"Nah, I'm good." They moved on to the next cabinet. "You still got a thing for her? Kelly, I mean? And don't tell me you didn't, we all knew."

Déjà vu, Matt had it. His gaze shot to his brother's profile and his brother's expression was almost as smug as Sabrina's had been. "Even you?"

Ty laughed over the whirring of the drill, then looked down at Matt. "You kidding? Especially me. *Especially* once I hit puberty—or it, me—and I was frustrated as hell that she treated me like a little kid."

"You were a little kid."

"My hormones would've begged to differ."

"Yeah, you were really suffering. Since, as I recall, even at that tender age you had your fair share of girlfriends. More than your fair share. *How* many bat mitzvahs did you get invited to that year?"

"Ah, but my heart belonged to a certain lovely redhead. However, since by then even I knew better than to encroach on my brother's territory, I let it go."

"Big of you. Since, as you say, you were nine." Ty shrugged. "Also…*territory?*"

His brother drilled in the next screw. "Whatever—"

"And second, Kelly wasn't *my* anything."

"Yeah, I finally figured that out." Ty dug another screw out of his tool apron, shaking his head. "And you had it all going on, too. Star quarterback, reasonably good-looking, *not* in the seventh grade…. Man, I hated you," he said with a grin, then frowned. "And yet you never did make a move, did you? God, you were dumb."

"I made a move," Matt said, earning him raised eyebrows. "Okay, I indicated I *might* make a move. You know how that goes."

"Not really, no. Subtle's not my style."

"So we've noticed."

Ty ignored him. "So you admit it, then? That you liked her?"

"Since we're talking a hundred years ago, yeah, what the hell."

"And what happened?"

"Not a damn thing." Because, as his sister had so succinctly put it, he'd been an idiot. Then again, if "everyone" supposedly knew about his interest in Kelly except Kelly, something sure as hell hadn't been working. "Signal boomeranged right back to smack me between the eyes."

"Well, that sucks." Ty climbed down from the stepstool, went to the old black fridge for a soda. Both dogs looked up. On the off chance a ham jumped out or something. "And now?" Ty said, popping the tab.

Matt shrugged. "And now is now."

"Meaning?"

"That you're looking for something that's not there?"

"Oh, it's there, all right. Seriously—why else are you renting her an apartment in your own house? And redoing the kitchen when you'd said you weren't going to for at least a year, because you *said* you weren't ready to be a landlord. Not to mention going with her to her ex-husband's funeral. Which, by the way, is sorta creepy. If you ask me."

"Which I didn't," Matt said, wondering if, in a previous life, the dude had been part of the Inquisition. "And did it maybe occur to you that I'm doing all this because for a long time Kelly was Sabrina's best friend, and she feels like family? And also maybe because I'm a nice guy who sees someone—three someones, actually—who could use a little support right now? They need a place to live, I have a place to rent. Some people might call that serendipity."

"Or stupidity—"

His brother's phone rang. As Ty answered it, Matt yanked open the fridge to get his own can of pop, praying the cold air would blast the heat from his face, the even hotter words logjammed in his throat. He loved his brother, but Tyler's habit of acting like his tough early years had made him some kind of life expert got on Matt's last nerve.

Especially when the punk's observations hit way closer to home than Matt would have liked—

"Yeah, I'll be right there. Crisis at the shop," Ty said as he slipped on his parka. "Gotta go back for a few. Don't mean to leave you in a lurch, though, so see you later?"

Matt took a deep breath, then nodded. Guy couldn't help being a buttinsky, that was just who he was. Also a helluva lot better at installing cabinets that Matt. "Yeah, that'd be great. Thanks."

"No problem." His brother whistled for Boomer—twice—before the dog woke up, staggered to his feet and reluctantly trudged after his master.

With a sigh, Matt slid down onto the tiled floor, his back propped on the pockmarked wall where a base cabinet would go. Alf roused herself enough to make the ten-foot journey across the kitchen, collapsing beside her daddy with her chin on his outstretched leg, sympathy shining in her golden eyes. Massaging the spot between the dog's ears, Matt let his head drop back, his brother's words replaying in his head.

Because for all Matt's good intentions, for all he really did want to help someone who obviously needed a leg up right now, this *was* stupid, *he* was stupid, for trying to act like some white knight. Especially since Kelly had made it more than plain that she needed, or wanted, a white knight in her life like she wanted lice. And you know what? Good for her. God knew there were any number of women out there who could learn from her example.

So why couldn't he simply step back and let her get on with it?

Matt exhaled. Loudly. Alf lifted her head, tail tentatively swiping the dusty floor. Fine, so he was attracted to her. Still. And again. He was gun-shy, not dead. And seeing the fire in her eyes as she'd talked the other night, watching her ripen into something strong and fierce and powerful right before his eyes…

Huge turn-on, that. Seriously.

However.

Matt forked his fingers into the dog's ruff while she licked his other hand. One thing about dogs, they were great listeners, but without that whole annoying, poking-their-noses-in thing.

"First off—" he looked down at his trusty companion, just to make sure she was paying attention "—neither one of us is even remotely interested in a relationship." Alf planted a supersize paw on Matt's lap, although whether in empathy or hope food might be involved, he wasn't sure. "Why? I'll tell you why. Because I screw them up, and Kelly's got her hands full getting her own head on straight. Right?" The dog barked. "*Damn* right. And the kids… Cooper…"

Yeah.

Alf hoisted herself upright enough to bestow a slobbery kiss across Matt's jaw. Disgusting, but loyal. Not unlike a lot of his buds in college, come to think of it. He'd only traded up was all.

Scrubbing away dog spit with his sweatshirt sleeve, Matt leaned back again, his eyes shut as he listened to Alf's panting in his ear, and firmly reminded himself that being lonely was no excuse for being an idiot.

But he still wasn't about to let Kelly go to this funeral by herself.

Chapter Five

Cooper guessed Mom had made a lot of the food on the table, since there was a whole bunch of stuff he didn't recognize. Actually, there was so much he could barely see Grandma's lace tablecloth underneath. How many people had she expected to show up, anyway?

Not that they would've fit. The place she moved into after Grandpa died…it was really little. So little, in fact, that when Coop and Linnie would stay here on the weekends after Dad moved in with Grandma, Linnie would sleep with her and Coop got the pullout sofa. Instead of sharing Dad's bed, which…nuh-uh. Even though he used to climb in bed with Mom and Dad on Saturday mornings when he was littler, and the bed would be all warm and smell like Mom's perfume, and Dad would tickle him with his whiskery face….

Coop cleared his throat, trying not to think about back then. About when everything had felt good. Before Dad lost his job and they had to leave their house, where Coop had had his own room and there'd been a big backyard, and Dad had promised that when he turned five, they'd get a dog. Except then everything went to heck in a handbasket, as Grandma would say.

He'd been so mad at first. At both of them. For breaking their promise or something. 'Course, he knew plenty of other kids whose parents got divorced, he just never thought it would happen to *him*—

Man, his brain felt as crowded as this table, crammed with all these half-finished thoughts. He almost wished he was little again, when he'd wake up in the morning and pretty much know how his day would go. When stuff didn't change like every five minutes.

Like how they were moving for real to Maple River to live in that apartment in Matt's house. So they'd be starting over *again*. Although at least he'd have his own room this time. And maybe he could go back to school, because it was getting kind of boring with just him and Mom. Also, Matt said he could hang out with Alf as much as he wanted, so there was that.

Coop put a little ham sandwich on his plastic plate, a few chips, but he really didn't feel much like eating. Except food usually made him feel better, so that was strange. But the past few days, it felt like somebody'd unplugged his stomach.

However, since he didn't want Mom or Grandma to get on his case, he took a bite of the sandwich, then scootched around a bunch of people to get back to the sofa. Only the bite had turned into this big, gloppy lump in his mouth, and he'd forgotten to get something to drink, and he didn't want to get up again because at least he was kind of invisible here. Seriously, if one more relative he didn't know started in about how sorry they were, about how brave he was, he was going to lose it.

He forced himself to swallow, trying not to make a face when he took another bite. Across the room, Mom was listening to someone Cooper guessed she didn't much want to listen to as she held Aislin, who'd passed out in her arms. Mouth open and everything. In a dark gray suit, Matt stood next to his mother like some kind of guard, and Cooper made that face, anyway.

Matt was okay, he guessed. But what was up with him coming to his dad's funeral like he was a real friend or something? Yeah, he and Mom had known each other when they were kids, but how close could they be if Coop had never even heard of him before last week? And now they were all going to live in his *house*...?

He hated that black dress Mom was wearing—it made her skin look way too white, like some creepy vampire. And this suit Grandma had dug up from somewhere, she said it'd been his father's when he was little, it didn't fit right. And was itchy as heck. A second later, like Mom could hear him thinking, she looked over, gave Coop a little smile. He tried to smile back but it probably looked totally fake.

Which made sense, since nothing felt real.

Like he'd gotten stuck in some weird dream. Partly because he still couldn't believe Dad was dead, but also because nobody was acting normal. Except maybe for Aislin, but she was only three, what did she know? Mom had warned him that at some point she'd probably ask where Dad was, but she hadn't yet, as far as Coop knew.

And what was he supposed to say if she did?

Blowing out a big breath, he looked down at his plate. Which was empty. Meaning now he was really thirsty. So he got up and went to the kitchen, ignoring Matt's eyes practically burning a hole in his back. Grandma was standing by the stove, holding a tissue to her nose, her eyes all puffy and red. Cooper pretended not to notice.

Except she noticed him, of course, swooping down to give him a hug. Usually Coop didn't mind—she was soft and smelled good, and hugs were nice—but now she squeezed him so hard it almost hurt.

"Ow! Grandma!"

"Sorry, sweetheart!" Making a funny little noise, she let go. "Don't know my own strength." She poked her fingers through his hair. "You need something, honey?"

He thought about asking for a soda—she would have totally given him one—but instead said, "Water?"

"In the fridge, help yourself." She went back to arranging another plate of food, the ends of her hair—brown, like Coop's—swishing around her shoulders. In the light coming through the kitchen window, he could see little silver streaks he'd never noticed before. Actually, she was really pretty—for somebody in her fifties, anyway—but today she looked…faded.

He supposed they all did.

Twisting the cap off his water, Coop returned to the living room as Matt was taking Aislin from Mom, and he remembered when the baby was really tiny and she'd cry and cry and cry until Mom would be crying, too, and Dad would come home and take the baby, singing to her in this really goofy voice….

He heard this strange sound, like somebody was being choked, only to realize *he* was making that noise, that he was crying like a little kid. And everybody was looking at him. *Everybody.*

He ran to his grandmother's bedroom and slammed the door shut, twisting the knob until it clicked.

* * *

"Coop?" Her heart pounding, Kelly softly knocked on her mother-in-law's bedroom door. Cooper had never locked himself into a room before, not even when Rick was acting like a total ass. "Honey? Open the door, I need to know you're okay."

"I'm fine. Go away."

Of course he wasn't fine, why would he be? His father had died barely a week ago, for heaven's sake, she was moving the kid away from everything he knew—

She sensed Matt come up behind her—speaking of unresolved issues—and heard Aislin's sleepy "Mommy?" Kelly reached for her daughter, except the little girl squirmed to get down...and made a beeline for the food table. Because...oh, God. When had she last fed her child?

"She's probably hungry—"

"On it," Matt said. "Anything off-limits?"

Kelly shook her head. Although, sadly, not hard enough to rearrange her brain cells. "Just make sure she doesn't take too large a bite...."

But he was already gone. And Linnie was already charming the pants off a dozen old aunts and cousins who needed a little sunshine on this gloomy day. Such tching and head-wagging she'd never seen. "To be taken so young," she heard over and over to poor Lynn. "Such a shame." At least Kelly, being the One Who'd Divorced *Him,* had been spared that much.

Of course, they didn't know the whole truth, that their "sweet Ricky" had turned into someone none of them would have known. That Rick wouldn't have known himself, if only he'd taken a good, long look in the mirror. Or his soul.

"I'm not going away, Coop," Kelly said, crossing her arms over the sucky black dress she'd finally found at the mall, hideous and hideously overpriced for something she'd never wear again. But at least the aunts couldn't say she looked like some hussy on the make. Well, they could, they could *say* anything they liked. And unfortunately Matt's insistence on coming along did provide them with a certain, ah, ammunition. Or, in ninetysomething Aunt Myrtle's case, a little thrill. Damned if Kelly didn't catch the old girl checking out Matt's butt. And giggling.

Anyway. What was true was true. And what wasn't wasn't.

And what was true right now was that her son, who'd shown virtually no emotion over his father's death in the entire week previous, had now locked himself in his grandmother's bedroom to, she presumed, have his overdue breakdown. So Matt's hyperactive pheromones could go play in somebody else's sandbox already.

Kelly leaned her now-aching head against the door. Hard, but cool. And solid. So solid… "Coop. Now."

Seconds passed before the lock finally tumbled, and Kelly released a breath. She scooted inside, pushing the door only partly shut behind her—it was stuffy as hell in here, Lynn kept the heat on full blast, yeesh—before tugging Coop down beside her on Lynn's comforter-swathed bed, wrapping him up tight in her arms to rest her chin in his curls. She'd been praising him so long for being such a big boy that she forgot, sometimes, how little he still was. That eight-year-olds weren't generally equipped to deal with this many life changes in such a short period of time, never mind what "they" said about kids being resilient. And here she was about to move him into yet another new home, his third in as many years.

A decision, she reminded herself as she inhaled his children's shampoo scent, she wouldn't have made if she hadn't truly believed it was for the best. For all of them. But would Coop see it that way?

He'd stopped crying, but seemed in no hurry to pull away. Which, despite the reason behind his reluctance, melted her heart. Moments like this would only become more rare as he got older, so she'd best treasure them while she could.

"Here—" Kelly sat him up, tugged off the ridiculous suit coat. "This thing is so not you." The coat tossed behind them, she pulled him close again. "So. Talk?"

His shoulders bumped. "You're busy."

Kelly leaned back, tapped his nose. "You come first, pookie-bear. You know that."

He groaned. And rolled his eyes. "Mom. You really need to stop calling me that." Teen-in-training, heaven help her. But at least the cloud had lifted for the moment.

"Sorry, no can do. Because you'll always be my pookie-bear. Even when you're all grown up and have kids of your own." At his horrified expression, she laughed. "Okay, so I'll only call you that when we're alone. Deal?"

"Do I get a vote?"

"Sure. But since I'm bigger, I get two."

Then he did pull away. But not from annoyance, she guessed. He sat forward, his feet dangling over the carpet. Standard-issue condo beige, Kelly noted. Boring but safe. Like the life she'd planned on having—

"I suddenly thought about Dad," Coop said softly, then looked up at her. "How he used to be. Before. And…it hurt. A lot."

"I know, sweetie. Believe me, I know."

He shoved up his glasses. "How come he changed so much?"

Oh, boy. "Well…I think your dad had a set idea about how things were going to go—with his life, I mean—and when they didn't go that way he didn't know how to adapt. How to go with the flow."

"Except…he *did* change."

"True, but—" Kelly thought a moment "—there are different kinds of change. There's being able to adapt, like I said, which is when something happens—good or bad—and you figure out new ways of coping. That's a good thing. A positive thing. Then there's reacting, which is almost always bad—a negative thing. Because then you feel so threatened by all the new stuff that you get scared. Or angry. Or overwhelmed. Which might make you take out your frustrations on other people. Which isn't cool."

"Like Dad did."

"Yes. Like Dad did. Although I really believe," she said, tugging Coop close again, "in my heart of hearts, that in *his* heart your father was the same person he always was. But he let fear and confusion blind him. And yes, that was very sad."

"But if you loved him, why didn't you help him?"

Her eyes burned. "I tried, sweetie," she whispered, rubbing his back. "Believe me. Grandma, too. We both begged him to go talk to someone who might have been able to make him feel better. He wouldn't do it."

"Why?"

"I don't know, honey. I really don't."

Coop sat up, frowning. "So, what? We're just…starting over?"

"I'm not sure we have a choice. Things aren't the same. We can either adapt…or not. But we still have each other, right? And we're taking all our old things to the new place. And you can see Grandma whenever you want. So what's important—that'll be the same. And hey." He swung his eyes to hers. "Alf?"

A small smile played around his mouth. *Gotcha,* she thought. Then his expression got serious again.

"But after that," he said, "no more changes, okay?"

"Not if I can help it. I promise."

And Coop released a huge sigh of relief.

They'd get through this, because you know what? Kelly was sick and tired of being life's bitch, of cowering before fate. But once this move was done, barring any other rude surprises the universe might want to vomit in their laps, she really did swear—no more changes. Coop had been through enough, *she'd* been through enough, to last them both for some time. Now her only goal was to reestablish a little peace and stability, to give both herself and her son a chance to regain their footing. Okay, *find* their footing.

And there was no place for handsome, overprotective cops in that scenario.

No matter how tempting that prospect might be.

Matt glanced over at Kelly, who was staring pensively out the passenger side window of Matt's Explorer as they drove back to Maple River. It wasn't particularly late, but it'd already been dark for a while. And by the time they'd helped Lynn clean up and then taken her out for Chinese—Kelly's idea, although Lynn had insisted on paying—they were all pretty zonked. Especially the kids, who were both sawing logs behind them.

"Warm enough?"

"Mmm-hmm," she murmured, then pressed her gloved hand to her mouth as she yawned. "Sorry."

"You look ready to pass out, too," he said softly, and she gave a little hmmph.

"There's an understatement," she said over another, longer yawn. Then she shifted in her seat, stretching out her arms. “Can’t, though.” Her hands fell to her lap. “Still have to make up the kids’ beds, didn’t have time before we left.”

“And nothing says you have to move in tonight, you can certainly stay at the house—”

“No. I mean, thank you, but…I think the kids are more than ready to be reunited with their things.”

“And you?”

Her eyes cut to his. “And me what?”

“You’re ready to…” Matt gestured lamely with one hand, searching for the right words. “To get on with… the next stage?”

“I am that,” she said on a huge sigh, her head falling back against the seat rest. “For their sake, more than my own. And hopefully this stage, as you call it, will last for more than five minutes.” She paused, then said, “I am so done with feeling as though I’m shepherding my children across one of those wobbly, rickety bridges suspended over a bottomless ravine. In the fog. Although at least now, maybe, the mists have dispersed enough to see the other side.”

Matt smiled. Ignored the impulse to reach for her hand. “I can make beds, you know.”

“What? No, Matt, you’ve already done so much—”

“We’re talking throwing some sheets on a couple kids’ beds, Kelly. Not staving off an alien invasion.”

She pushed out a short laugh. “What are you, the Energizer Bunny?”

“I could say the same about you. Look at how much you’ve dealt with in the past week, including a move. Not to mention today. You’ve gotta be drained by this point. Hell, I’m drained, and it wasn’t… Well. Personal for me. So I’m making the beds. Deal with it.”

“God, you’re bossy,” she said, but he caught the smile. “And I’m too tired to argue. Heck, I’m almost too tired to breathe. Let alone talk." She shot him a fleeting, apologetic look. "You mind?"

"As long as you don't start snoring, too, I'm good," he said, and she *hmmphed* another little laugh through her nose.

"Message received," she said, then crossed her arms and leaned her head against the window, her eyes drifting closed. Only then she added, "I really am grateful."

"For?"

Yawning again, she snuggled farther down into her seat. "Everything. I've gotten so used to doing it all myself…." Her eyes still shut, she reached over to briefly squeeze his forearm. "You're a good friend, Matt Noble…."

Touched by her sincerity, Matt glanced across the seat. But she was already asleep, her breath gently stirring a delicate, coppery coil of hair that had drifted across her mouth. And something stirred inside him, not so gently, a peculiar mixture of sympathy and annoyance, admiration and yearning. Not lust, exactly—although that curl across her mouth was definitely rattling loose a few bolts of his control—but definitely an ache. To touch. To hold.

To be something she didn't need him to be.

That he wasn't sure he could be.

Huffing a sigh of his own, Matt focused on the dark, but far less trafficked, back road she'd recommended they take, weaving through the townships and farmland that gave lie to their proximity to one of the most heavily populated areas of the country. She had no idea, of course, that he'd overheard a good chunk of her conversation with Cooper earlier. He hadn't meant to eavesdrop, of course, only to quickly peek in to make sure both mama and son were okay. But he'd gotten the gist—Coop's plea for no more changes, Kelly's assurance there wouldn't be.

Boy, could he understand that.

After everything they'd been through, it was only natural that they'd want things to finally settle down. For a while, at least. Turbulence might be character building, but it was really tough on the soul. Which Matt not only knew from personal experience, but also from witnessing the toll constant upheaval took on kids with stressful home lives. Hell, on anybody's. Meaning his guess was that Kelly's promise was as much to herself as it was to her son. And who could blame her?

So it was all good. That the attraction was one-sided, that is. Made things a lot easier for everybody, right? And yet, as he drove, listening to the kids' soft snorts and groans in their sleep, Kelly's even breathing beside him, something like contentment spread through his chest that she'd called him her friend. And meant it.

That she obviously trusted him.

It also startled him to realize that, right now, at this moment, what they had was already head and shoulders above what he'd had with his ex. With any girl or woman he'd even been involved with, frankly. And that felt good, too. Like maybe he was finally growing up, he thought with a smirk.

A few minutes later, they pulled up in front of the house, all of his passengers still zonked. He looked over at Kelly, slack mouthed as she slumped against the window, and he thought about that conversation, how patient she'd been with Coop, and a wave of tenderness shunted through him. He *could* tell himself he was just feeling brotherly, but he'd be lying. He could, and did, however, tell himself to get over it.

"Hey," Matt whispered, briefly touching her hand. She jerked awake with a soft gasp, frowning at him for a second. "We're…" *Home,* he almost said, thinking, *What the hell?* "Here."

"Oh." She blinked a few times, then let out a soft laugh. "Wow, I was really out. Whew."

Behind her, Coop yawned and unbuckled himself from his booster seat, fumbling for the door handle as Matt got out, went around to the boy's door.

"No, I'm good," Coop said, not quite pushing past Matt, but close enough, before slightly staggering toward the side entrance to the apartment. From behind his living room window, Matt could hear Alf going berserk. A much more raucous display than she'd ever put on for him, for sure, he thought as he rounded the car again to take the sleeping toddler from Kelly's arms.

"No, it's okay—"

"Good God, what do you feed this kid?" he said with a mock grunt. "She weighs five hundred pounds. Coop?" When the boy turned, Matt tossed him the keys. "Black one's the top lock, red's the bottom. Go on and say hi to your dog before she explodes. What?" he said to Kelly's confused, still half-asleep frown as Aislin slumped against his shoulder, her curls tickling his cheek. And, yeah, a not-so-little twinge zinged through him that this had been how he'd seen his life by now—wife, kids, dog, house. What did they call that? Oh, yeah…a *life*.

"*His* dog?" Kelly said, frowning, curls wafting every which way in the night breeze, glimmering in the porch light, her skin so smooth and pale and…

"Can you *hear* that?" Matt said, tearing his gaze from Kelly's mouth. The frown, too, but mostly the mouth. Spotting Coop, Alf went into overdrive, trying to hurtle herself through the triple-paned picture window. Matt grinned. "Yep, definitely Coop's dog now. Come on, let's get those beds made…."

They all trooped into the house and through to the living room, where Coop and Alf indulged in a boy-and-beast lovefest, rife with giggling and dog spit. Still holding the little girl, Matt nudged on the thermostat, then let his gaze slide to Kelly. Hands shoved in the pockets of her black, calf-length dress coat, tears glistened in her eyes.

"After today, of all days…he's laughing."

"I think that's one reason my folks always had animals in the house," Matt said softly, hiking up the baby as he watched the two, now wrestling on the worn beige wall-to-wall carpet he'd yet to change out. Next project. After he repainted. And got rid of the prissy grandma drapes. "Especially dogs. Hard to be scared or angry or confused in the face of a dog's love."

"I remember that." She snorted. "My mother loved to complain about all the dog hair on my clothes when I'd come back from you guyses house." Matt chuckled at her uncharacteristic New Jersey-ism as she added, "I take it there was a dog when you and Sabrina arrived?"

Almost forgotten images flooded his brain. "After the accident, Bree wouldn't talk. To anyone, not even me. We'd sheltered with another family for a few days. They were kind enough, I suppose, but everything seemed… I don't know. Like I was watching a movie about my own life."

"I can imagine," Kelly said quietly, slipping out of her coat to fold it across her arms.

Matt glanced over, caught the understanding in her eyes then turned back to the wrestling match. "All I remember is trying to get Bree to talk to me, how scared I was that she wouldn't. Even though everybody kept telling me not to worry, that eventually she would. But I didn't believe them. Couple days later, they moved us to the Colonel's. Why, I have no idea. But there was this dog…"

In his arms, Aislin hauled in a deep breath; smiling, Matt breathed with her, realizing she smelled like Kelly's perfume. "A golden retriever, I think. Or something close.

Soon as we set foot inside, she—Sally—hustled right over to us, wagging her tail, smiling the way goldens do. Then she started nudging us until we started petting her. And Bree…"

Matt blinked, remembering. "She got down on her knees and hugged that poor dog's neck like her life depended on it. Then she looked up at Mom and whispered, 'What's her name?'" He grinned over at Kelly. "She hasn't stopped talking since," he said, and Kelly laughed.

"Since he was two," she said, "Coop's wanted a dog. And we'd always planned on getting one. Bought a house with a large, fenced-in yard, even. But Rick thought it best to wait until Coop was older, and I didn't disagree with him. Then, of course…"

She shrugged, then sighed. "I'd forgotten how full of *joy* dogs are. How much they simply love for the sake of loving."

"That they do," Matt said as Aislin woke up enough to stuff her thumb in her mouth. And although she didn't seem in any hurry to leave Matt's shoulder, he imagined Kelly was ready for them all to be in bed so she could collapse in hers.

"Here," he said, shifting the toddler back into Kelly's arms. "Where's the sheets and stuff?"

A tiny smile toyed with her mouth. "In a box labeled 'sheets and stuff' in the master bedroom. Aislin's are pink and Coop's are blue." Her shoulders bumped. "All my creative energy goes into my cooking, what can I say?"

"So I'm guessing your sheets are white?"

Surprise flashed across her face before deepening into a blush. "Ivory, actually. But I'll make my own bed, thank you."

Damn, she was cute. Although probably not a good time to tell her that. Or any time. No sense in poking that particular beast.

"Go sit, then. I'll be right back."

Fifteen minutes later, he'd made all the beds—yes, including Kelly's, she could deal—and tried not to react to how barren the place looked. No furniture except beds and dressers, a dinette set she'd scored at some furniture warehouse at the outlet mall the day before. He knew *stuff* didn't define *home.* That the kids—and quite possibly Kelly, for that matter—didn't care. But he'd been in her childhood house a couple times, with Sabrina, probably, and he knew Kelly had grown up with nice things. And she deserved nice things now.

Not that this was any of his concern.

Matt returned upstairs via the shared laundry room in the basement to find Kelly practically asleep on his sofa—which was no great shakes, either, now that he took a good look at it—while the kids played with the dog. At his appearance, she pushed herself upright, offering him a sleepy smile. Her dress was a maze of wrinkles and her hair looked like the kids had played in it. But it made her look *real,* you know? Like somebody who maybe wasn't afraid of a little dirt.

Except when her eyes didn't quite meet his, Matt realized she sure was afraid of something.

And he had the very distinct feeling that something was him.

What the hell?

She hadn't been asleep, exactly, but definitely in that floaty, peaceful place where, even though she could still hear the kids, her thoughts had been taking her on some very interesting little trips. Then she saw Matt standing there, all smug smile and dimples, and that lovely, floaty bubble went *pop!*

"Done?" she said, trying not to look quite so much like

a zombie. A zombie, she realized as she glanced down, with no fashion sense whatsoever.

"Everything but the mints on the pillows," Matt said. "But only because I'm fresh out."

"You are such a goof," she murmured, smiling in spite of herself, as she surreptitiously tried to smooth out the relief map stretched across her lap. But at least the day was almost over—hallelujah. "Okay, you two," she said as she shoved herself to her feet, wobbling a bit in her high-heeled boots. "Bedtime!"

Face flushed, curls wild, Coop hugged the dog, and Kelly's heart melted. More. "Can Alf come, too?"

"Oh, honey… She's Matt's dog, remember—?"

The dog woofed, then plopped her butt next to Coop, as close as she could get without sitting *on* him. Then she lowered her head and gave Matt The Look: *Please, can I spend the night with The Boy? Pleeeease?*

Kind of matched the one on Coop's face, actually.

"Up to you, Mom," Matt said. "Although, actually, letting her hang out here's not a bad idea—she's a great watchdog. Unless you'd be more comfortable with me staying here…?"

"And leave your sister all alone in that huge house?"

"Believe me, now that I've got running water again, I'm only there for Pop. Because woe betide any burglar dumb enough to mess with Abby," he said, and Kelly laughed. Then sighed.

Because she got it. She did. More to the point, she got *him.* And was guessing, from the hot, sweet look in those dreamy brown eyes, she could have him. Aaany time she wanted. For the moment, anyway. 'Course, that could be her poor, neglected libido playing tricks on her, too. So she smiled and said, "We'll be fine. We've been on our own for the past two years, remember? Besides which, before that Rick was away a lot for his job. Although—" her gaze slid to the dog "—if you really don't mind leaving Alf here…?"

"Not at all." But she heard in his voice, the sacrifice he was making. Saw it when he squatted to ruffle the fur around the dog's neck, his God-I-love-this-dog grin when the thing slurped her tongue across her master's rough cheek. He stood, turning to Coop. "If she bugs you in the middle of the night just let her outside, she'll come right back. You good with that?"

"Yeah," Coop said, beaming, his curls bobbing when he nodded.

This I can give him, Kelly thought as she slipped her coat back on, then herded everyone to the front door. Cold air rushed in when Matt opened it, laced with the promise of a new snowstorm, the first itty-bitty flakes already dotting her face. And the baby's, apparently, judging from her shrieked, *"Snow!"* followed by Coop's "I am so gonna make a snowman tomorrow!"

"If there's enough, go for it. Here," Kelly said, handing Coop the apartment key; boy and dog barreled out onto the porch, Aislin pounding the boards right behind them. An instant later all three were bouncing around in the front yard as though they'd had jumping beans for dinner.

"Yaaay!" Coop said, arms outspread as he whirled, and Kelly pressed her hand to her mouth, tears stinging her eyes that something as basic as snow, with a giant dog galumphing around them, was working magic on her little boy.

Coop grinned back at her. "Can we stay outside for a couple minutes? Please?"

"I suppose. But don't you dare lose that key!"

"I won't, I promise!"

He grabbed his sister and spun her around, their laughter mingling with the dog's excited barking, and Kelly laughed as well, then lifted her head, breathing in the clean, snow-scented air.

"A foot, maybe, they said," she said, almost reverently. "Lucky us, right?"

Frankly, she'd been avoiding looking at Matt, afraid of what she might see. Or, worse, what he might. Poker faces were not her strong suit. Even so, between the gentle snow and her kids' laughter and frankly being too tired to give a doodly-squat, when Kelly finally did turn to him she somehow felt…at peace. In control. Then he said, "I made up your bed, too," and the peace shattered, severely wounding the control in the process.

"Even though I told you not to."

"You can rip it apart and remake it if you want," he said, and she looked away again. In the light from the streetlamp, fat, lazy flakes sparkled and twirled. As did Aislin, who then stumbled into the dog and went *plunk* on her butt…and let out a scream of laughter that made Kelly chuckle, too. Then she sighed.

A really heavy sigh that got a questioning look from the man standing beside her, close enough to get a whiff of leftover aftershave.

"What was that all about?" he said.

"Nothing. Really."

"And if that's true, you'd be the first woman on earth to actually mean it…and what the hell is she doing here?" he said as his sister's seen-better-days Subaru pulled up in front of the house. A second later, Abby emerged, androgynous in her jeans and UGGs, a ridiculously long scarf coiled several times around her neck and shoulders.

"Hey, guys!" she called, and kids and dog all bounded over to her, where the two wee humans regaled her about the "great big snowman!" they were going to build tomorrow. After Abby promised that, sure, she'd help, she stomped up the porch steps.

"Out of hot chocolate mix, figured I could score some here…." Her brow slightly knotted, she looked from Kelly to Matt. "Everything all right?"

"Uh…yeah?" Matt said. "Why wouldn't it be…?"

"Mom?" Cooper yelled over. "We're freezing, so we're going inside—"

"You guys want some hot chocolate?" Abby yelled back. "Stupid question, of course you do, you're kids. Hang tight, I'll get it and be there in a jiff—"

"No, it's okay—" Kelly began.

"I was leaving, anyway," Matt interrupted, but Abby shot them a look that would have quelled God.

"Whatever I interrupted," she said under her breath, "you need to finish. And don't give me any crap, either one of you." Then she vanished inside the house, emerging almost immediately with the Nesquik, giving them both a you-may-now-proceed wave before trundling down the steps.

"She was a lot cuter when she was little," Matt said, and Kelly smiled.

"And I think that's called selective memory. She was a bossy little twerp, even then."

"True."

Silence pulsed between them for a few painful seconds before Matt said, "So. *Is* there something we need to finish?"

"Not that I can see," she said, and started down the steps, hearing Matt follow, the *boop-boop* of his car unlocking…and suddenly years of keeping quiet, of keeping the peace, exploded in Kelly's brain, and she whipped around and said, "Why *did* you make my bed when I told you not to?"

* * *

His car door already open, Matt turned, frowning. What the hell? "Because I'm a nice guy?"

"Of course you are," Kelly said on puff of air, then sank onto the bottom step. In the snow.

Matt shut the car door. Leaned against the fender, his arms crossed. "Is there a problem?"

She yanked her coat closed, then linked her arms around her knees. "Yeah," she breathed out. "You."

"Excuse me…?"

"Because you *are* a nice guy. Too nice, maybe. And it's not that I'm not grateful for everything you've done—I mean, the apartment kitchen? I was good with it the way it was, you didn't have to redo it—"

"Actually, I did. Trust me."

"Fine, whatever. But—" she rocked back and forth for a minute, like she was trying to work up to whatever she had to say "—I can't let you keep doing stuff for me. Not that I don't like it, or…or don't appreciate it, because I do. Really. But letting other people take care of me… I've done that all my life. And now…I don't dare. Not anymore."

"I see," Matt said. Not that he did, but it seemed the prudent thing to say.

"Because that's what got me into trouble. Before, I mean. With Rick. It's how I was raised, to let the man handle all the important stuff, to make all the decisions…." She shook her head. "And didn't that blow up in my face?"

Matt pushed off the fender to go and sit beside her, but her hand shot out, stopping him. "No. Stay over there. Please." When he settled back against the car, swiping snow off his hair, she said, "Rick promised to take care of me. I was good with that, and so was he. We each had our role and all that. And for a long time, things were good. But…"

She lifted her eyes to his, blinking in the snow. "It was

all an illusion. Like…like a stage set for a castle wall. Looks real enough, but push it too hard, and *wham.*" She smacked the heels of her palms together, then tucked her hands back under her folded arms. Matt thought her teeth might have been chattering. "Wasn't until things started going south between us that I finally realized I had to man up. And fast. For the kids' sake, especially. And amazingly enough, I discovered I was perfectly capable of taking care of myself, and my children, of doing a heckuva lot more than I'd believed I could. Except…"

From the basement, they could hear, faintly, the kids laughing, the dog barking. A slight smile curved her mouth. "I'm not out of the woods, yet. I still feel…vulnerable."

"For God's sake," Matt said quietly, "anybody would, in your situation. It's been a rough week. Hell, from what you told me? A rough couple years—"

"I know that. Just as I know there will always still be times when I'll need support from other human beings. Same as anybody else. That nobody can get through this crazy life entirely on their own. Which is why I brought the kids to your dad's house. The problem is…" She laughed, a shaky, embarrassed sound that made Matt hurt for her. "I mean, you're a prince. Seriously. And I get that you can't help being who you are. What you are. Unfortunately I can't help being who I am, either. What *I* am. And what I am right now—and maybe forever—is someone who doesn't dare let herself get sucked in by someone like you." She almost smiled. "You are too good, Matt. Too kind and giving and, well—" the smile stretched a little more "—noble."

"You say this like it's a bad thing."

"But that's just it. For me, it is. A very bad thing. Because this nasty little voice keeps telling me I'm worn out and stressed and oh, my *God* it would be so easy to let you take care of me. To let you be The Man. But…I can't grow if people don't give me room to do that."

"People meaning me, I take it?"

"Meaning anybody. But since you're the one standing here…"

Her voice drifted, but her gaze ka-plowed into his. Only for a second, but that was one intense second before she broke the connection, looking off to the side.

Huh.

God knows, Matt was no mind reader. Especially when it came to women, if his marriage was anything to go by. But it wasn't like he could come right out and *ask* if there were more to Kelly's objection than her simply not wanting him to play Sir Helps-a-lot, was it? Not without probably making things worse. And, anyway, random zings happened. Ninety-nine percent of the time they meant nothing. And he sincerely doubted this was that one-percent exception. On either of their parts. So that was one dog he was not about to wake up.

But he could ask… "So if this is such a *problem,* why are you here? Living in my house?"

She rubbed the toe of one boot for a moment, then looked up again. "Because the schools are great and the rent is good and because I know you won't let the kitchen faucet drip for three weeks before you finally fix it. Probably."

At that, he chuckled. "No, I definitely won't let the faucet leak for three weeks—"

"Not that I couldn't fix it myself, but that's not my job."

"Right—"

"And also because I'm not about to let my own issues get in the way of what's best for my children."

No. She wouldn't. Again, Matt thought about that overheard conversation, the way she interacted with her kids. What she'd risked for their sakes—

His cell phone buzzed. Frowning, Matt plucked it off his belt, read the text through the snow, looked over to her. "It's Abs. You ready?"

Nodding, Kelly stood, still hugging herself. "Did… What I said… Did you understand what I was getting at?"

"That you need your space? Sure." Still, he heard the Colonel's voice in his head, to watch out for her. Not that he needed any prodding. "Which you can have right after I walk you around to the apartment."

"For heaven's sake—"

"So sue me," he said, hands crammed in his jacket's pockets. The wind picked up, making him blink in the snow. "I've got this thing about looking out for people. Always have, from the time I was little."

"I remember that," she said softly, coming closer. "Even though Ethan was older, you were the one who'd keep an eye out on the younger kids. Especially the fosters."

He felt his mouth stretch as they started around the house. "Pop used to say I must've been a border collie in another life."

That got a little laugh. "Yeah, I can see that." Kelly made a circling motion at her own face. "Around the eyes, especially," she said, and Matt snorted.

But when they reached the apartment's door, he touched her arm, making her face him. Droplets of melted snow streaked her glasses over cheeks reddened from the cold and another wave of tenderness shunted through him. Entirely inappropriate though it may have been.

"I can stay out of your way, if that's what you really want. But if you need me—for anything—I'm here. Got it?" Then he walked away, feeling honorable as hell.

Or something.

Chapter Six

By mid-February, life had finally settled into something resembling a comfortable routine. Although, Kelly supposed, as she inched forward in the elementary school pick-up lane, Aislin's tuneless singing behind her competing with the cold, relentless rain pounding the van's roof, that depended on how one defined *comfortable.* Or *routine.*

Yes, she had her new health-department-approved catering kitchen and had lined up enough events to keep the wolf at bay for some time. And she'd found a fabulous part-time babysitter in Mrs. Otero, her always cheerful next-door neighbor. Matt had also been as good as his word, leaving her alone. Although she could tell, when they ran into each other—which they frequently did, since he was around all the time, working on the house and such—that it was killing him not to ask how she was doing, if there was anything *he* could do. But so far he'd kept his promise.

Except for the texts. The text giving her Mrs. Otero's

number, or the lead on the kitchen—honestly, the man had more connections than a sorority sister—or telling her that his brother Tyler coached Coop's age group in soccer, if she was interested.

Oh, and giving Coop Ty's old bicycle. The kid had outgrown his first two-wheeler a year ago, but with everything else going on Kelly hadn't gotten around to replacing it.

Yeah, the dude was her angel, all right. An angel who refurbished twenty-year-old Power Rangers bikes so they looked practically new. Especially to her slightly weird third-grader who actually thought it was cool that the bike was old.

Her slightly weird, but very brave, third-grader who'd announced he wanted to try going back to school before Kelly even broached the subject. Three weeks in, things seemed to be going well on that front, too, thank God.

Through the downpour drenching the entire East Coast, she saw Coop slaloming through a million other kids toward them. She waited…waited…then punched the side-door button at the precise moment that allowed the child, but not the deluge, access. *Bam.*

"How was your day?" she asked once he was buckled in.

"Okay. We had a math test. Where's Alf?"

Kelly eased into the line of cars circling toward the street. "You think I'm gonna bring a hundred-and-twenty-pound dog out in this," she said over Linnie's singing, "you're nuts. And how'd you do on the test?"

"I got a 95." Kelly gave him a thumbs-up between the bucket seats. He giggled, then said, "Can I ride my bike?"

"In this weather? As if."

"It's only rain. And I got a 95!"

"No."

"I'll wear my helmet and pads—"

"No."

"Fine," the kid said on a "Moms, yeesh" sigh. "In other news…I made another friend. Tad. I think he lives close, can he come over sometime?"

"You bet. Any homework?"

"Nah, 'cause I already did it. But I've got a library book to read and do a report on…."

For the rest of the short drive back to the house, Coop nattered on about PE—dodgeball—the assorted critters living in his classroom and the sucky food in the cafeteria…could he *please* take lunch? And the *normalcy* of the conversation was such a relief Kelly nearly cried. So what if it was boring? Right now, boring was good. Heck, boring was heaven. She wanted to wrap herself up in boring, marry it and have its babies—

"Hey—what's Matt doing on the roof?" Coop asked as they pulled into the driveway.

Being an idiot? Kelly thought, unbuckling her seat belt as her firstborn exploded from the car. Although the rain had downgraded from monsoon to miserable, still not exactly ideal weather for tramping around on two-story roofs. What the hell?

Matt looked down as the wind puffed out his gray poncho, making him look like an evolving jellyfish. And yet still sexy. Go figure.

"Leak," he yelled down. Not smiling. Understandable, since poncho or no, he had to be soaked to his skivvies.

"Oh, no," Kelly yelled back, lamely, trying to nudge her brain past *skivvies, soaked* and *Matt* in the same thought. She'd have better luck herding cats. Or, in this case, a fascinated eight-year-old into the house.

"Coop!" she called, trying to coordinate springing Aislin from her car seat while putting up her umbrella, a move that, alas, she'd yet to master. With any grace, at least. "In case you hadn't noticed, it's pouring! Get inside!"

"Jeez, Mom! I'm not gonna melt!" Hand still visoring his face, he glanced over. "And no, I'm not gonna get sick, either. Germs make you sick. Not weather."

Briefly, Kelly mourned the removal of "You'll catch your death!" from the Top Ten Mom Threat List, only to decide to skip logic—outdated or not—and go straight to "Because I said so."

"Cooper Eugene Harrison! Inside! *Now!*"

Seconds later, the warm, dry, beef-stew-scented apartment greeted them like an old friend. Amazing, she thought as she wiped her fogged glasses, then peeled damp—or, in Coop's case, sodden—clothes from little bodies, how quickly the place had begun to feel like home. Yep, warm, and dry, and safe—

Alf's sudden crazed barking nearly gave Kelly a heart attack.

"Someone's knocking!" Coop yelled as Aislin, curls a blur, shoved past the dog, yelling, "I got it, I got it!"

"No, you don't got it, little girl," Kelly said, scooping her eager little door-person into her arms before checking the peephole. Even though, given the dog's frantic whining and scratching at the door, who else would it be? And explain to her how Matt Noble was the only person in the world who, through a peephole, didn't look like something out of a freak show? "We do not open doors unless Mama says it's okay," she said into those curls. "Got *that?*"

"Uh-huh. 'Zit okay?"

"Since it's Matt, yes," she said, setting the child on the floor and thinking, as she unlocked the dead bolt, steeling herself against all those humidity-plumped pheromones, so much for safe. "So you may open the door."

After much tugging and grunting—heavy door, good to know—it finally swung open. And there he was, looking good. Wet, but good. And clutching a large plastic bag with a toy store name on it.

"Hi, Matt," the baby said, doing her half twisting, half bouncing Linnie wiggle. As was the dog, who was yodeling as though she hadn't seen Matt in years. "Mama said I couldn't…open the…door unless she said it was okay. But then she did. 'Cept…" Midwiggle, Linnie frowned up at Kelly through the wild curls, and she moved "trim Linnie's hair" up on the to-do list. Because three-year-olds really shouldn't look like Medusa. "You didn't say if he could come in."

Kelly laughed. "Yes, sweetie. He can come in."

Aislin faced Matt again. "She said it was okay."

"Thank you," Matt said solemnly, then crossed the threshold. But only as far as the tiled entryway. Kelly grabbed the towel she'd just used on the baby and tossed it to Matt, vaguely regretting that she couldn't strip *him* down to dry him off—

"Thanks," he said, wiping his face one-handed and draping the towel over the doorknob, then holding out the bag. "I bought these for the kids weeks ago. Except with everything that happened I forgot about them. And since you're all home—"

"Mama! Mama! What is it?"

Kelly opened the bag, only to feel her breath catch when she saw the LEGO set. Crap. So she pulled out the sock monkey first—in rainbow colors, no less—and handed it to Aislin, who gasped, squealed then rushed Matt to hug his thigh. "Thank you!" she mumbled into his soggy jeans, then said, "I have to go show him to everybody else!" and tore down the hall.

Then, her chest still knotted, and with no way to give Matt a heads-up, Kelly handed the bag to Coop.

"This was so thoughtful, Matt," she said, hoping against

hope her son got the message. Still, she braced herself. Except after pulling the huge box from the bag, Coop slid down the wall to sit with it in his lap, *awestruck* being the only word to describe his expression.

Kelly's eyes filled; she cleared her throat and prompted, "Coop?"

The boy bit his bottom lip, then whispered, "This is…" He clumsily hauled himself to his feet, then looked at Matt. "It's awesome. I've wanted this one forever. Thanks."

"Glad you like it," Matt said, obviously releasing a breath of his own. "If you need help, let me know. My brothers and I built hundreds of these things when we were kids."

"Thanks, I will." Then, to Kelly, he asked, "C'n I go get started on it now?"

"Of course, sweetie."

The dog, naturally, went with. A moment later, she heard Coop's door close, then Matt quietly said, "You're crying?"

Perceptive guy, that Matt.

Sniffling, Kelly went into the living room to pluck a tissue from a dented box on the coffee table. "A few years ago—" she shoved up her glasses to wipe her eyes, then blew her nose before facing Matt again "—there was…an incident. Involving Coop's father and LEGOs."

Matt blew out a heavy sigh. "Oh, God, Kelly, if I'd known…"

"How could you have? Heck, LEGOs and little boys go together like milk and cookies. And obviously it's all good now, so—"

"What happened?"

Kelly glanced down the hall to make sure Coop's door was still closed, then lowered her voice. "Lynn had given Coop one of those humongous sets for Christmas, one way too advanced for a five-year-old." Her mouth twisted. "Or a man whose life was unraveling, although I didn't know it at the time. I had to take Aislin for her six-month checkup, so I left Coop with his dad. I returned an hour later to find a explosion in my living room, Rick in a rage and Coop sobbing harder than I have *ever* heard anybody cry."

At Matt's muttered swear word, she nodded. "Yeah. Exactly. And before I could ask what happened, Rick stormed out of the house, leaving me with a hysterical little boy *and* a screaming baby, since naturally Linnie picked up on the distress. It took me forever to get the kids calmed down. And a lot longer than that before I found out Rick knew he was about to lose his job. But thinking I couldn't handle the news, he held it in. And trying to assemble the stupid LEGO set sent him over the edge."

Matt gave her one of those trenchant looks. "Was that the…beginning?"

"Of the end? Yes." The real end, at least, when she'd finally realized that once a dream starts unraveling, there's no putting it back together. No matter how badly you might want to. "Coop was petrified, cowering on the floor beside the sofa. And my first, horrified thought was that Rick had hit him. And looking back, I'm not sure he wouldn't have if I hadn't come home when I did." The pain flared into fury. "I don't care how unhappy you are, you do *not* take it out on a child. I didn't let Rick back in the house that night. And I never, ever left Coop alone again with his father."

"Good for you," Matt said, his eyes never leaving her face, where a tight smile stretched her mouth.

"I was so angry and scared, it hurt. It *still* hurts. All those nasty what-ifs…" Kelly shuddered, raking her hand through her curls. "But even though there were no more rages—for a long time, anyway—the damage was done. Coop's trust in Rick… It was as shattered as those LEGOs, whether I fully admitted it at the time or not. And Coop refused to play with them from then on, even though he'd been hooked on the things from his first DUPLOs when he was a toddler. So when he pulled that box out of the bag..." Her lips pressed together. "It could have been disastrous."

"Meaning you haven't bought LEGOs for him since then?"

"Would you have? Given the circumstances?"

A second or two passed before Matt crossed his arms. "Well, as you said, it's obviously all good now. And even if it hadn't been, my feelings would have survived, believe me." He snorted. "Ethan's oldest girl is a total pain to shop for," he said, and Kelly smiled. "Anyway," he said, "about the roof..."

Then he shut his eyes, breathing in deeply.

"What?" Kelly asked, slightly alarmed.

Eyes still closed, Matt inhaled again, then sighed. "I've been trying to ignore that incredible smell, but..." His eyes opened. "Damn. What *are* you making?"

"Beef stew," Kelly said, relieved. That she didn't have to call 911, at least. "Nothing fancy."

"From *scratch?*" he said, sounding so pathetic she nearly laughed.

"Well, I didn't slaughter the cow or grow the veggies, but yeah. So what were you saying about the roof?"

"The roof, right." Palming the back of his head, Matt huffed a breath. "I was hoping to hold off until spring before replacing it, but it's worse than I thought. Another rain like we had today..." His hands slammed back to his waist. "So the roofers'll be here next week, if the weather holds. I don't think the noise'll be too bad down here, but figured you'd appreciate a heads-up."

"Oh. Okay. Thanks."

And if she'd expected him to nod and leave, she was

wrong. Instead he pocketed his hands and said, "So how's Coop doing in school?"

"Good," she said, as it hit her—the guy was lonely. An almost alien concept to her, since, between the kids and work and everything else, Kelly hadn't had time to be lonely in… Gosh. Forever.

Or so she'd convinced herself.

"You going back to your dad's tonight?" she asked, even though what she really wanted to do was sign him up for online dating. Or something. Anything. Because that hound-at-the-pound expression was not a good look for him. Or, alas, her.

"No, actually," he said on a whoosh of air. "He returned this morning. Complete surprise, he'd said he was staying much longer. Can you imagine, *voluntarily* returning to Jersey from Florida in February? Anyway, so I'm back in residence. Not that you wouldn't've figured it out on your own soon enough—" He lifted his head again. "Man… that smells *so* good."

And she thought the dog was a beggar. Then again, considering everything he'd done since she'd moved in, including staying out of her way—and he *had* brought the kids gifts, which was very sweet and totally unexpected—she *supposed* the least she could do was invite him to dinner. In fact, she *supposed* it would be rude not to.

Of course, she *supposed* she could pretend she was dense. Or ungrateful. Or a bitch—

For crying out loud, this was nuts. The man had kept his promise, she felt totally safe around him—okay, mostly safe—and they were all adults, here—

"Um…the stew won't be ready for a couple hours yet, but if you don't have plans…"

Oh, dear. Man was watching her so intently she was surprised steam wasn't rising from his wet clothes. "Unless you count channel surfing until I keel over from boredom…nope. No plans. No plans at all."

And this would be so much easier if he weren't so gosh-darn cute. "Then why don't you come for dinner?"

After what felt like an eternity of more steamy staring, he said, "You sure?"

"Of course," she said, all bright smile and whatnot. Hard to do and not breathe in those pesky pheromones. "Wouldn't have invited you, otherwise. So…sixish?"

He grinned. Not a sly grin, or a sexy grin, just…a Matt-being-Matt grin that warmed her through and scared the bejeebers out of her at the same time. Because it was the very innocence of that grin that could lead to some very not innocent goings-on, if she didn't keep her wits about her.

"What can I bring?"

"Not a thing. I made pies earlier."

His pupils got *real* big. "Pies? *Plural?*"

"Yep. Apple-cranberry and rum custard."

He pressed a hand to his chest. "Swear to God, if I had a ring on me I'd ask you to marry me right now. Is rum custard even legal?"

"Just barely," she said, thinking those eyes were going to be the death of her. Speaking of things that shouldn't be legal. "But fair warning, they're experiments. And I am no stranger to culinary catastrophes."

There went the grin again. "So I should bring ice cream as backup?"

"Wouldn't hurt. Especially since there's no way the kids will touch the pies."

He laughed, tingling her to her tootsies all over again, then whistled for the dog. Coop's door opened and Alf loped down the hall, only to put on the brakes when she realized what was up. Chuckling, Matt squatted, his hands on his knees. "I'll bring you back later. I promise."

She could have sworn the dog sighed before going to her master…and that Matt gave her a wink before he left.

Testing times, she thought this was called.

As Matt finished off his second piece of the rum custard pie, he thought, *Nope, nothing even remotely terrible about this.* Or the evening, for that matter. Yeah, he was feeling pretty damn mellow right about now. The stew had more than made good on its olfactory promise, and the kids' conversation—you haven't lived until you've heard a toddler's and a third-grader's very different takes on *Monsters, Inc.*—had kept him laughing the whole time they'd been at the table. And if promises of another sort were not on the menu, it was still nice simply getting out of his own head for a couple hours.

Afterward they'd moved into the living room, where Matt had stretched out across the brightly patterned area rug angled across the light-colored laminate floor. Coop was in the far end of the room, vanished into the land of LEGOs. And Aislin, who'd attached herself to Matt like a tick, had brought at least a dozen books out of her room and plunked them on the floor, before calmly plunking herself at his hip and handing him one, then another, and another after that. He'd been reading aloud—stopping every few lines to allow for the little girl's running commentary—between bites of the heaven that was Kelly's pie.

One book done, Aislin immediately replaced it with another. "This one's my favorite, it's about dogs." At the word *dogs,* Alfie lifted her head from where she lay alongside Kelly's thrift-store-find sofa, a bluish-greenish tufted-velvet number that had probably once been the showpiece in somebody's grandmother's formal living room. Keeping the sofa company were a deeply cushioned chair the color of a ripe tomato and a curvy rocker with lime-green cushions. A huge, and very welcome, change from the original bleakness—

"Sometimes books about dogs are sad," the little girl was saying, "but I don't like those ones. This one's funny—"

"Linnie, for heaven's sake," Kelly said, returning from the kitchen with another piece of pie for herself. She folded one leg underneath her butt and sank into the corner of the sofa, actually looking somewhat relaxed. Certainly a helluva lot more than earlier, when she'd told him about that horrendous day with Rick and the LEGOs.

At that point it had taken everything Matt had in him not to hug her, showing his support like Mom had always done with all her kids—meaning any kid who set foot in her house, short-term or long. Like he remembered his own mother doing, even if the memories were pretty worn and faded by now. Words were tricky, words could trip you up. But touching… That'd been around since long before humans figured out how to move past grunting.

Not to mention touching was how a man expressed what he was feeling when his brain and tongue felt disconnected from each other—

Smiling for her daughter, Kelly jabbed the fork at her. "He's already read three—that's plenty."

"And I promise," Matt said, facing Aislin, both to disengage from that wayward thought and tweak one of those adorable curls, "we can do this again," and the kid's dimpled grin melted his heart even as it stirred up all the old regrets. Then he returned his gaze to Kelly, and something else stirred. Yes, *that.* But more than *that* was the truth: that, against all common sense and all sense of honor, the pull was still there. Meaning right now he couldn't help but appreciate the way her hair glowed against the blue sofa. How her position, despite her baggy jeans and loose sweater, delineated a curve or two that hadn't existed a month ago.... "If Mama says that's okay."

Kelly snorted around the tines of her fork as she sucked off a blob of custard, and Matt clenched his teeth. "You might want to be careful what you're offering, she loooves books," she said, and Matt thought, watching that fork as it slid back into her mouth, *You might want to be careful about what* you're *offering.* Except she wasn't. Not even subconsciously. And he knew it. But, hey. Fantasies happened. "Doncha, sweetie?" Kelly said, sliding the fork out of her mouth again, and what little mellow he had left disintegrated.

"Uh-huh," Aislin said with a vigorous head shake, clutching the dog book to her chest. "But Mama doesn't read as many as I want her to." She leaned forward and whispered, "'Cause sometimes she falls asleep."

"Aislin Marie! Honestly!"

Chuckling, Matt glanced over at Kelly again, catching the cute little pink blotches peeking out from beneath her glasses frames. Occasionally he wondered what she'd look like dressed up—in something other than that butt-ugly funeral dress, that is—but there was a lot to be said for her hey-this-is-me-deal-with-it wardrobe of jeans and sweaters and jackets. Lots of black, he'd noticed, he supposed since that was what she wore for work. But with that red hair and her pale skin, black was good. Hell, black was hot.

And a little more mellow floated away....

"And, anyway, little girl," Kelly said, "it's almost bedtime. So go get your jammies on, I'll come help you brush your teeth in a minute—"

"Awww..."

"No, *awww*-ing. Now git." With a dramatic sigh, Aislin heaved her small self to her feet and tromped down the hall to her bedroom as Kelly said to Coop, "You, too, honey. It's later than I thought."

"Mom! Since when do I go to bed the same time as Linnie?"

"Since tonight, 'cause it's late. And no arguments. You know I have to get you guys to Grandma's early so I can go to work. And I do not need to deal with a sleepy cranky-pants tomorrow morning. 'Kay?"

"'Kay," Coop grumbled, unfolding himself from the floor and giving the partly built set a longing look before trudging off to his own room.

Matt curled forward into a sitting position, close enough to pat Kelly's knee. That got a look—big surprise, right?—but not quite the look he would've expected. Oh, he caught the "watch it, bub," but mixed in with a little...what? Curiosity, maybe? Then again, could've been the light from the lamp by the sofa flashing off her lenses.

"I'll clean the kitchen while you herd," he said, getting to his feet.

"Don't be silly." Kelly stood as well, brushing pie-crust crumbs off...the front of her sweater. "You're a guest, you don't have to—"

"Kelly?" Matt clasped her shoulders, rock hard under his hands, saw her pupils widen. Her lips part. In surprise, most likely. With no small difficulty, Matt reminded himself that he was a gentleman, that the Colonel had drummed into all his sons' heads that a real man respected women. Controlled his impulses. Always. Yes, even when that man's mouth felt electrified with wanting to kiss the stuffing out of the woman right in front of him, when he itched to soothe away the tension tightening her forehead muscles, those shoulders. In any number of intriguing ways. "Hush," he said quietly, as much to himself as to her, then released her and went back to the kitchen, where the cold, congealed leftover beef stew seemed to taunt him.

Or at least dampened his ardor enough for his brain cells to remind him that if this was him being *protective,* he was doing a piss-poor job of it.

When Kelly returned, Matt was sitting on the edge of the couch, his jacket across his knees as he leafed through a home décor magazine. Frowning.

"It's one of my weaknesses," she said, heart hammering as she moved around the living room gathering toys, coats, plates. Telling herself she hadn't sorta hurried the kids through their bedtime routines, sorta hoping Matt would still be here when she came back out. The *why* part of that she hadn't quite worked out yet. "They're mostly the same every month, but there's something secure about that."

"This where you got the ideas for in here? These colors?"

Her arms full, she glanced up. "Um…maybe?"

"I like it. Not that I know squat about this stuff—" he waggled the magazine, then tossed it back on the coffee table "—but far as I'm concerned, you decorate as well as you cook."

Kelly blushed, only to then sneeze—loudly—when a stray curl tickled her nose.

Chuckling, Matt blessed her. Then said, "You sneeze like a teamster."

"Awful, isn't it?" Heading toward the wicker baskets on the shelves on the other side of the room, Kelly caught a glimpse of the sparkling kitchen. And her heart went *ba-dump.* "Wow."

"Between the Colonel and my mom, we all learned to clean. Early and often."

"I remember that. Thank you. Or them, whoever."

"No, thank *you.*" He paused. "Kids get to sleep okay?"

So sad that she couldn't tell if he was simply being polite or giving her a cue. Sadder still was that she had no idea which of those she wanted it to be. Or whether she should fib, say they were still awake—thus mitigating the hokey-pokey potential—or tell the truth, see how that played out. She'd meant what she'd said, about needing her space, to continue figuring out who she was. What she needed. And yet…

Going for option number two, she said, "Out like lights, both of them. They're both definitely sleeping better now that things have…calmed down."

Kelly dumped the toys and straightened, finally tucking that damn curl behind her ear where it couldn't cause any more trouble. Matt was on his feet, hands in pockets, his jacket tucked into the crook of his elbow, and she thought, *All righty then, problem solved.*

Except, alas, in her head, where self-preservation and loneliness were locked in mortal combat. Yes, loneliness. Because all that stuff she'd thought earlier? About not having time for *lonely?* Utter and complete hooey.

"Um…would you like to take some pie with you? Can't eat it all, would hate to throw it out."

Matt smiled. A soft smile, barely visible through the scruff. Kelly duly—but not dully—considered that scruff, about how sensitive her skin was, and her heart started banging so hard she nearly passed out—

"Can't have that, God knows."

What? Oh. "No," she said. "Can't have that." Goodness *gracious,* her sternum was going to hurt like hell in the morning. "Well. Okay. Let me get that packed up for you…."

Kelly turned toward the kitchen, letting out a little gasp when she found herself somehow cradled to his chest.

Oh, she thought, smelling him, wanting to *inhale* him as she listened to his lovely strong heartbeat, soaked up how amazing those arms felt folded around her, and she nearly cried, it felt so good and it had been so long, and heck, yeah, she missed this....

Then reality cleared its throat behind her, and she thought, *Right.*

Also, *damn.* But *right* was louder.

With extraordinary effort she pulled away, imagining her expression was about as defined as one of Aislin's scribbled masterpieces. Matt, however—standing with his thumbs in his pockets, almost slouching, for crying out loud—looked as though a bomb could go off behind him and he wouldn't even flinch.

"Your call," he said, and Kelly did flinch.

"Wh-what?"

"Whether I go or stay." He smiled. "And before your head explodes, I don't mean 'stay' as in 'overnight.' Or even what 'overnight' implies. I know you don't want that, and even if you did—" he paused, giving her a moment for that to sink in "—I wouldn't suggest it, anyway, given... given where we both are in our lives right now. Especially not with the kids around. No, I mean 'stay' as in hang out. Talk. Watch TV. Hell, play a board game, if that floats your boat. Whatever friends do."

"Oh," she said, wondering why she didn't feel more... relieved. Instead of, say, like a bird had just crapped on her head—

"And I'm guessing," Matt said, his voice all low and rumbly and, not to put too fine a point on it, sexy as hell, "there's enough going on behind that 'oh' to fill a Russian novel."

After a very brief detour involving the incongruity of Matt and Russian novels in the same thought, Kelly finally lowered herself to the overstuffed chair, gripped the corded cushion's edge and said, "You should probably go."

"If that's what you want..."

Want. Such a simple word, so many interpretations...

She dropped her face into her hands, suddenly so weary she wondered how she was still upright. Well, mostly. Then, on a huge breath, she let her hands fall to her knees and met that steady brown gaze. "Okay, here's the thing—part of me wants you to stay, too. The part...I can't trust. The part that got me into so much trouble before. Having you come to dinner, with the kids, is one thing. Being alone with you..." She frowned. "What do *you* want?"

"From you?"

"Sure."

"Right now? Your company."

"And that's all?"

Matt chuckled. "The truth? No. But you don't strike me as the kind of woman who fools around just for fun. And that's all it would be."

"For whom?"

He hesitated, then said, "Either of us, I imagine."

"Because your ex broke your heart?"

He actually flinched. "How...?"

"Abby, first. Then Bree. Yes, we've been talking again. So you've got no one to blame but yourself for that one. And it's pretty obvious," she said gently, "that they're both worried about you."

"Sisters," he muttered, and she smiled. Then, very slowly, he slipped his jacket back on. "Well. Thanks again for dinner."

"Um...you're welcome?"

Matt called the dog, stretched out on the floor in front of the hallway. "Alf? You coming?" She lifted her head, seemed to ponder his question for a moment, thumped her tail once then laid her chin back on her front paws.

"Why am I not surprised?" Matt muttered, then opened the door, banging his hand on the edge a moment before saying, "Watching you with Coop and Linnie tonight, all I could think was that those kids lucked out, getting you for their mother. I also remember—" his eyes darkened "—how you used to be with the kids we fostered. And Abby. It's why I…" He stopped, his mouth pinching shut for a moment before he said, "You deserve more than a little *fun,* Kelly."

Stunned, she could only gawk as he dug in his pocket for his keys, then turned to leave. Only he'd barely set foot outside when something like rage surged through her.

"Hey." Matt pivoted back, frowning. "So do you, turtle brain."

Then she slammed shut the door, the doo-doo in the 'do feeling ratcheting to epic proportions.

Especially when she realized, with a huge sigh, she still had all that pie….

Chapter Seven

In his living room, Matt laid the paint roller in the pan on the newspaper-covered coffee table and grabbed his can of cola off the windowsill—the prissy sheers having gone to the Big Window in the Sky a week ago—and stretched out his back as he frowned at the newly painted wall. Kind of a brown-paper-bag color, which looked better than it sounded. With white trim it'd be okay, he guessed. Some random lady at Home Depot—who he'd finally figured out was coming on to him—tried to sell him on either this gray the color of wet cement, or an acidy green that had reminded him of something he'd pitched from his fridge the other night. She insisted the colors were very popular these days. Sophisticated, she said. Ugly was what they were. Not to mention depressing as hell.

A moment later, the feeble early-March sun scooted out from behind a cloud and lit up the still-wet wall, and the color brought to mind fresh-baked peanut-butter cookies.

He'd take that over mold any day, he thought with a slight smile as his gaze landed on the picture album the Colonel had left on the family room coffee table the other day, now splayed open on Matt's.

Cola in hand, Matt crossed the room to lower himself to the edge of the sofa, the corners of his mouth tucked up as he leafed through the album again. He wasn't sure why he'd lugged it back to his house—nostalgia was usually lost on him—but the damn thing had sucked him right in, all those pictures of his brothers and sisters as kids. Of the people he'd called his parents for most of his life, his mother laughing, the Colonel close by, his eyes always on her, never the camera. Of skinny baby Abby, her flyaway blond hair floating around a perpetual glower. Like she'd been born tough.

Of Kelly, grinning shyly between Matt and Bree at middle school graduation, her ballooned red hair tickling Matt's nose; as a wild-haired Thelma to Bree's headscarfed Louise that next Halloween; a shot of her asleep in one of the Adirondack chairs out back, one-year-old Abby sacked out on top of her, both of them with their maws wide open.

She had no idea he'd taken that picture, Matt thought with a slight smile. Let alone that it had found its way into the family album—

Her nose smashed to the bottom the front door, Alf started woofing and whining and wagging; a moment later Matt heard the side door to Kelly's van slide open, the kids' chatter as they disembarked. He got up and sidled over to the window, his mouth stretching again when Aislin headed straight for a puddle left over from yesterday's rain and he heard Kelly's exasperated "Don't even think about it!" as she grabbed the back of the little girl's puffy coat. Beside her, Coop yakked away, swinging his backpack. Matt thought maybe the kid's face looked thinner. He seemed happier, too. Okay, so maybe "happy" was overstating it. But definitely less *un*happy, which must have been a huge relief for his mother.

It'd been two weeks since that dinner in her apartment. Far as he could tell she seemed to be getting along okay, doing whatever it was she did during the week when Coop was at school, heading out with the kids almost every Saturday dressed in her caterer duds, often returning without them late that night—sleepovers at Grandma's, she'd explained as they exchanged mixed-up mail one day. And if Matt couldn't relax until he heard the van chug back into the driveway on those nights, that was his problem. Not Kelly's.

Otherwise he hardly ever saw her or the kids except from right here, watching her herd her brood in or out of her van, or Coop ride his bike when the cul-de-sac was dry enough. Or when Alf asked to go play with her boy, so Matt would take her down to the apartment and he and Kelly would exchange a minute or two of carefully pleasant conversation, and he'd see glimpses of the bright-eyed girl from the album, from his resurrected memories, overlaid with the gutsy mother of two that girl had become.

Yeah. Gutsy enough to throw his words right back in his face.

After that dinner, he'd lain awake most of the night. Fuming, for the most part, even though he had no reason, or right, to be mad. At Kelly, especially. But then, somewhere around two in the morning, the annoyance burned away enough for him to at least entertain the idea that maybe she had a point. Not that Kelly knew the details about his and Marcia's breakup—nobody else did—but aiming blindly or not, she'd hit the target dead-on.

Because far as he could tell, it wasn't his fault his marriage had failed. That wanting to take care of someone didn't make him the bad guy. And that, hell yeah, he deserved good things. Same as he'd said to Kelly. Same as Jeanne had said to him, to all of them, more times than he could count.

Including Kelly, as he recalled.

Everything she'd said about needing to find her own footing... He got that. Respected it, even. But that girl in the photos... He'd liked what he'd seen, and heard, even back then. Even if he hadn't really understood what it was he liked so much. And now she was back and all grown up, and the grown-up version fascinated him even more—

He realized she was looking right up at the window, her forehead creased. Chuckling at himself, Matt backed away from the window.

Only to immediately think, *The hell with this.*

"Shoes off!" Kelly yelled, kicking off her own at the door as the kids rushed inside ahead of her. It had warmed up just enough to melt the ice from the last storm, turning Maple River into Mudville. Disgusting.

Not nearly as disgusting, however, as her realization, when she'd noticed Matt at his window, that, (a) she yearned for him as much as ever—if not more, that whole absence-makes-the-heart-grow-fonder thing a truism for a reason—and, (b) that despite being ever so grateful he was giving her *the space she'd asked for,* it also galled her that he was. Because, see (a).

The urchins dashed to the kitchen for a snack, never mind that Aislin had devoured a stick of string cheese, an entire cut-up apple and three peanut-butter crackers an hour earlier. At this rate she'd be taller than Kelly by next week.

As would Coop, Kelly thought as she wrenched open

the plastic container filled with her "special" cookies—whole-grain oatmeal with raisins, pecans and dried cranberries. "Only one, it's spaghetti night," she said, ruffling first one curly head then the other before pouring glasses of milk to go with.

Grabbing her own cookie, Kelly leaned on the kitchen side of the tiny breakfast bar, watching her kids watching some cartoon on Nickelodeon…and watching her thoughts meander down dangerous paths. As in, for all she knew Matt was shagging some other woman senseless on a regular basis. A thought that made her, well, sad. And…itchy.

She broke off a huge chunk of cookie and crammed it in her mouth.

Of course, she *didn't* know what—or who, or if there even was a who—Matt was doing. She did know, however, that she missed him. Which was sad. *So* sad, in a what-the-blue-blazes-is-*wrong*-with-me? kind of way. Because that little business about just having a little *fun*... Yeah. Kept calling to her as loudly as that pint of premium double-chunk chocolate-fudge ice cream hidden from the kids in the back of the freezer: the temptation to indulge this…this *ache* that would not go away. If anything, the whole giving-her-space thing wasn't working worth beans.

And she didn't only mean sex. Although, okay, fine, that was a huge part of her confuzzlement. Again, sad. Because…one touch? *One?* And *boom,* her body was all, *Oh,* yes, *more please?* Like being bitten by a freaking vampire, for God's sake.

But, heck, that was about missing something that hadn't even happened—she shushed the sniggering little *yet*—as opposed to all that he-man protectiveness crap she'd sworn she would never, ever, ever get sucked into again. Ever.

Because she knew Matt had been watching her this

whole time. No, correct that—watching out for her. Watching *over* her.

Exactly like an angel is supposed to do, she thought on a smirk as her doorbell rang. She stuffed more cookie in her mouth. Because it was there and she could and she was queen of her domain.

Coop checked the peephole, opened the door. "Matt!" he said, gleeful. Yeah, she strongly suspected her son missed the man, too. Not to mention how much the dog, who was about to explode with bliss, missed her kids. So there, in all his Latin-Jersey-cop glory—a deadly combination if ever there was one—the man stood beside his combusting dog, his gaze sliding right to her masticating self. And he did that corner of the lip lift that got everything buzzing, and she thought, *Doomed, I so am.*

Then again, since avoidance wasn't working now any more than it had in her marriage, maybe it was time she bucked up and met it head-on. Like the way you trained a dog to ignore distractions by putting them in various, potentially aggravating situations until they no longer reacted. Worth a shot, right?

Still chewing, Kelly shoved up her glasses and held out the container. "Cookie?"

Because if you can't beat 'em, feed 'em.

Matt had no idea what he was doing. Why he was here. Much less why "It's actually sunny and not freezing, you guys wanna go for a walk?" came out of his mouth. As, it should be noted, he ambled over to Kelly and took the cookie. Took a bite. Nearly died from sensory overload. Behind him he heard a pair of enthusiastic "Yays!" from the short people, who were probably as tired of the sucky, yucky winter as he remembered being when he was a kid.

Still munching away, Kelly glanced up at the kitchen

window. Not wearing black today, but a button-front sweater in a dull purple—for her, practically a circus color—that went really great with her hair.

"Not much daylight left for a walk," she said, which got a chorus of "Aww..." from her munchkins. She turned back to the kids, brushing crumbs from her hands. "I didn't say we couldn't go—"

"Can I take my bike?" Coop asked, and Kelly sighed. Matt could tell she wasn't a huge fan of Things with Wheels That Might Hurt Her Child, and she'd bought the kid enough protective gear to outfit a New York Ranger, but she was doing her best. "Yes, you may take the bike. But it'll get dark soon. And cold. So we'll have to make it quick."

Matt could handle quick. Sure, slow was better, he was a big fan of slow, but if your only option was quick, you went with it. And were grateful.

Kelly's gaze flicked to his, like she knew exactly what he was thinking. Damn. Was he really that transparent? Aw, who was he kidding, he was a guy—might as well stick a megaphone in his skull and bypass speech altogether.

Feeling like an idiot—if not a jerk—Matt was briefly tempted to say, "On second thought..." and book it the hell out of there. Instead, a few minutes later everybody was bundled up and off they went, Alfie playing Nana to the kids' Peter and Wendy about fifteen feet ahead of him and Kelly. And Matt would have been lying if he said he didn't think about what it would be like, going for a walk with his own family, his own kids. His own wife. Annoyance pinched that he'd been *so* close.

Only not as close as he'd thought. Obviously.

And don't go getting any ideas about this one, either.

He glanced over at Kelly, hands balled in the pockets

of her down coat, her gaze nailed to her children. He wondered what she was thinking. Wondered why the silence between them didn't particularly bother him, even though he guessed she was only doing this for the kids.

"So whatcha been up to?" she suddenly asked, shoving her hair behind her ear.

"Finishing the upstairs, mostly. Um…sorry about the sander the other day, thing makes a god-awful racket—"

"No, it's okay. I took Aislin over to Lynn's, we had lunch."

"Oh. Good." Matt coughed into his gloved hand. "How's Lynn doing?"

Her shoulders bumped. "Who knows? I mean, on the surface, sure, she's fine. But women—" a damp breeze shunted down the block; Kelly hiked up her hood around her neck "—we're pretty good at hiding our pain. Because God forbid we worry anybody, right?"

Matt thought of the Colonel, who'd barely mentioned his wife for more than a year after her death. Of how Matt's refusal to admit how badly the divorce had shaken him had nearly cost him his job. How he still fought talking about it. "You think only women do that?"

Her eyes cut to the side of his face before facing front again. "You're right. That was unfair." A puff of air crystallized in front of her face. Ahead of them, kids and dog stopped to cross the empty street, Coop grabbing his sister's hand even as he straddled the bike. Matt could feel Kelly relax—as much as she probably ever did, anyway—before saying, "I have clearly spent way too much time inside my own head."

"Yeah. I know how that goes." He paused, then said, "Look, I stayed out of your way because I thought that's what you wanted. What you still want, for all I know. But… if you'd like somebody to talk to, to get *out* of your head,

I'm a good listener." He smiled. "Ask Bree, she nearly talked me to death when we were kids. Until she found you. And…what was his name? That nerdy guy you two hung out with?"

Kelly laughed. "Cole Rayburn. Oh, my gosh, I haven't thought of him in years. Is he still around?"

"Cole, right. And I have no idea. Anyway…Bree didn't confide in me so much after that. At first I was relieved. But then I realized how much I missed…her trust." He paused. "I know a lot of people. And I've got family coming out of my ears. But I don't have many friends. Real friends, I mean. Not sure how that happened."

"I know what you mean," she said after a moment. "Weird, huh?"

"Very."

They reached the small park at the end of the block, the rays from the setting sun gilding the lifeless winter grass, the bare-limbed trees. Kids and dog took off toward the playground, where Coop dumped the bike in the grass. Matt led Kelly to a west-facing bench nearby, plopping right down on the gouged wood. Kelly, however, made a face, then stripped off one glove to test the seat—making sure it was dry, he assumed—before joining him. Tongue lolling, Alf plodded over and crashed beside them.

With a soft laugh Kelly bent to pat the dog's back, then sat up again and crossed her arms. "I wasn't much of a confider. At least, not then." Her lips curved. "Bree did enough of that for both of us. Then I grew up and there really wasn't anybody to talk *to*. Even when I wanted to."

Matt studied the side of her face. "Meaning, your husband?"

"Yeah."

"Thought you said—"

"Controlling isn't the same as protecting," she said quietly, smiling when Aislin yelled, "Look at me, Mama!" from the top of a slide barely as tall as her brother. Kelly waved, then sighed. "Only then I didn't know the difference. And by the time I finally woke up, we already had a kid."

"*A* kid?"

Another smile flitted across her lips. "Linnie is more precious to me than my own life, but the circumstances surrounding her...happening weren't exactly fortuitous. I'll spare you the details," she said with a sad twist to her mouth, "but when I realized I was pregnant—and after I got over being shocked, and yes, angry—" she pulled a cuffed hat out of her pocket, yanked it down over her head "—I convinced myself that our focusing on this new little blessing would rejuvenate our marriage." More mouth twisting. "*Wrong.* Looking back... Even a year before Rick actually lost his job, he was struggling. Business was down, so his sales were off. Not his fault, but he didn't see it that way. And it's next to impossible to love someone else when your own self-esteem is in the toilet."

Matt sat back as her words sank in. Because despite what she'd said about her own self-confidence struggle, it was obvious how much *Kelly* loved those kids.

Like she'd read his mind, she said, "When I was pregnant with Coop, I was petrified. That I'd screw up, or wouldn't be able to live up to your mother's stellar example. Ironically, Rick was thrilled. Because at that point, everything was going exactly as he'd planned it out. When his world—our world—fell apart, so did he...and I finally learned how to fly. Or at least flutter from tree to tree. Before that, though..."

She looked at Matt. "The fears didn't automatically vanish the first time I held Coop. But the *love*..." Blinking, she faced the playground again. "That love... It was so much stronger than I was. Almost…a presence, a…a conviction that didn't come from some limited, precarious place inside me, but from something, or some place, far bigger than I could even comprehend. And I somehow knew that presence or whatever it was would carry me through, and over, my own fears." She let out a soft, shaky laugh and said, "And now you probably think I'm bonkers for sure."

"Not hardly," he said at last, then twisted to lean one elbow on the bench back's top, watching the breeze toy with her hair. "You ever say that to your husband?"

"No," she sighed out. "Or anybody else, for that matter. Because I couldn't've put those feelings into words if I'd tried. Not then. And by the time I did, I knew Rick wouldn't understand. And I didn't want to put a wedge between us."

"By being honest?"

She sort of laughed. "Yeah."

"A problem you clearly don't have with me."

There was a pause, then she said quietly, "I don't have anything to lose with you. If you think I'm nuts—" she shrugged "—no biggie."

For the moment, Matt let that go. The *biggie* was that she'd trusted him with something she hadn't told the man she'd wanted to hold on to so badly; she'd shielded him from who she really was. He could only hope she'd eventually realize how bass-ackward that was.

Even as the voice said, *Your turn, bub,* and he squelched a sigh.

He knew how doubtful it was that anything would happen between them, no matter what he said or did. Or even if it was right. Maybe he finally felt ready to break free of all the crap clogging his brain about Marcia and his marriage, but for more than that? He wasn't sure, to be honest. He did know, however, that you couldn't force things to work out.

And, boy, how.

But sometimes all you could do was take that first step and not worry about what came next.

"Okay," he said, sitting forward again with his hands linked between his knees. "Fair exchange, since I never told anybody this, either…but after my divorce, after I'd turned myself inside out trying to become whatever the hell Marcia thought I was supposed to be, after a year of thinking *I'd* failed—" he faced Kelly's slight frown "—I found out she'd been cheating on me practically the whole time we'd been married."

"Oh, Matt," Kelly breathed out. "Seriously?"

"Swear to God."

"And you really never told anyone else? Not even Bree?"

"I think Bree suspects. But oddly enough she's never pried, and I certainly never volunteered the information. Because knowing Bree, she would've hunted Marcia down and ripped her hair out," he said, and Kelly snorted. "Anyway…that's why I worked all those extra hours. To keep myself from thinking about what a damn fool I'd been."

"And why on earth would you think that?"

Matt felt his mouth pull tight. "Maybe I misread her signals, I don't know…but I'd gotten the feeling she wanted to *feel* wanted. So that's what I did. The flowers, the gifts, the whole nine yards. And at first, it seemed to work. She certainly acted flattered, anyway. And I like doing stuff for people, you know?"

"So I noticed," Kelly said, a smile in her voice.

He sighed. "Except I guess… Well. After we'd been married for a while, she said I was crowding her. Although I'm now thinking she meant that as in, *three's* a crowd. And I was number three." He sat up straight again, his gaze fixed on the play area. "There's one mistake I'll never make again. Being there for someone, sure. That's just me. But next time—if there ever is a next time—it's both parties meeting halfway or nothing. My pushing days are over."

Kelly was quiet for a moment, then reached over to slip her gloved hand into his. When he gave her a startled look, she said, "Whatever. She was the fool. Not you. And right now? I wouldn't mind doing a little hair pulling myself."

Then, their hands still linked, she faced the kids again, her face glowing in the last, brilliant rays of the setting sun. And although both sun and hand disappeared a moment later, Matt figured he'd be glowing, too, for some time to come.

Why, he'd figure out later.

Going *to* the park had been fine, Cooper thought as he biked behind the grown-ups, Aislin clinging to Matt's back like a little monkey. Chattering like one, too. Gosh, he remembered when she couldn't even talk. Now she never shut up, unless she was asleep.

But, anyway, it'd been fun and all, while they were there. But now things felt…strange. 'Course, it always felt strange this time of day, not dark but not light anymore, either. Except he knew the time of day had nothing to do with how he was feeling, but seeing his Mom and Matt holding hands…what did it mean?

Because if Mom and Matt decided they liked each other and stuff, that'd be another change, when things had barely started to feel normal again. Except… Going back to school had been a really big change, too, and that was going okay, right? And he liked their new place, and Matt's family, and, well, Matt. But he didn't know Matt. Not well enough to think of him like a dad, anyway, a thought that made his heart start thumping like crazy.

He supposed he could ask Mom what was going on, but grown-ups weren't always real good at telling the truth.

Like how Mom had pretended for so long that everything was okay between her and Dad when even as a little kid, Coop had known it wasn't. So did it work the same way in reverse? That they'd pretend nothing was going on and then one day suddenly say, "Hey, we're getting married?" Just like his mother had said, "Hey, we're getting divorced?" Okay, she hadn't said it like that, but whatever.

Of course, there was stuff Coop still hadn't told Mom, either. Stuff maybe he'd never tell her. But that was different, because—

"Coop? Wanna talk to Grandma?" He jerked to attention to see Mom holding out her phone. Wow. He'd been thinking so hard he hadn't even heard it ring.

"Hi, Grandma," he said, as he put the bike out back then went inside the apartment. Where Matt was, too, he noticed.

"How are you doing, sweetheart?"

"Okay. We went to the park with Alf."

"Alf…? Oh, Matt's dog?"

"Yeah." Leaving the others in the living room, Coop went down the hall to his room—it was kinda small, but at least it was all his—and shut the door. "Can I tell you something?"

"Of course, honey, you can tell me anything."

Coop looked over at the finished LEGO set, up high on a shelf where Linnie couldn't get it. "I saw Matt and Mom holding hands."

"I see." Grandma got quiet for a moment, like she was thinking. "And did that bother you?"

Coop stretched out on his bed, frowning up at the star

stickers Mom had put on the ceiling before he'd had a chance to tell her he was too big for that sort of thing now. "Doesn't it bother *you?*"

"Oh, honey… People touch each other—like holding hands—for a lot of reasons. You…could be reading something into it that's not there."

"And what if I'm not?"

He heard her blow out a breath. "Okay. I love your mother. You know that, don't you?"

"Yeah."

"And your father, may he rest in peace—he put her, he put *all* of us, through a lot, those last few years." She paused and said softly, "Including you. Right?"

Coop's chest got all tight feeling, but he nodded. Then he remembered Grandma couldn't see him. "I guess."

"Yeah, well, I *know.* It was awful, and I'm not going to pretend it wasn't. And Matt…" He heard her sigh. "Honey, listen to me. I only met him the one time, when I wasn't exactly in a good place. But even then I was impressed that he came all the way out here to your father's funeral so your mom didn't have to deal with it by herself. That's a good man, sweetheart. A nice guy. And you know what? Your mother could maybe use a nice guy in her life. And so could you and your sister."

"But it's not right! Dad *just* died!"

Coop jerked. What the heck? Why should that even matter, especially considering what all else he felt…?

"Except," Grandma said, real quietly, "aside from the fact that your mom and dad hadn't been married for a while by then, if you think about it…the daddy you remember from when you were little left us a long time ago. Do…do you understand what I'm saying?"

Tears stinging his eyes, Coop nodded. Because hadn't

he said exactly that to Mom, the day of Dad's funeral?

"Y-yeah."

"Aw, sweetheart… I didn't mean to make you cry. But you know something? I'd like to think your dad's free now. From whatever scared him so much. The thing is, though… so are you. Free, I mean. Your mom, too. Look, I'm not there, I have no idea what's going on between Matt and your mom. Could be nothing, for all I know. For all *you* know. But there's good things waiting for you, I promise. So promise *me* you'll keep your heart open so you don't miss them. Will you do that for me?"

Coop sucked in a breath that shook his whole body, then nodded. "I'll t-try."

"No. *Promise.*"

He sort of smiled. "Okay. I promise."

"Good boy," Grandma said. "By the way, did your mom tell you? I'm picking you and Linnie up on Friday to spend the whole weekend with me. And to see your new apartment. So make sure your room's clean, kiddo."

"I will. I love you."

"Love you, too, baby. See you soon!"

Cooper ended the call, then sat on his bed, frowning. And wishing he could wind his life back to when he was four or something, when everything felt so much *simpler.*

Giving the spaghetti sauce a quick stir, Kelly smiled at her daughter's belly laugh in the living room, where Matt—back against the sofa, his legs stretched in front of him—had turned the kids' army of stuffed toys, led by General Rainbow Monkey, into a production worthy of Steven Spielberg. Voices and all. And the *drama*... Oh, my gosh. Clearly those Russian novels had left an impression.

The same way Matt, despite her druthers, was making an impression in her life. Her heart. Weak as water, those druthers. It made no sense. How could she feel this threatened by someone so utterly nonthreatening? It was like being scared of the Easter Bunny. If the Easter Bunny had dreamy dark eyes and dimples that would not quit and a laugh that made her womb weep.

Then again, clearly Matt's ex had felt threatened, too. By what? His love and goodness and generosity…?

Coop slogged into the kitchen to hand back her phone, looking far too emo for an eight-year-old. Or anyone, for that matter.

"What on earth did Grandma *say* to you?"

Her child shot her A Look, then released a breath. "Nothing," he said with a shrug, and it was everything Kelly could do not to grab the front of his hoodie and intimidate him with the dripping spaghetti sauce spoon until he 'fessed up. But all she'd get for her efforts, probably, was a sauce-stained hoodie, so she restrained herself.

Restraint, she thought, her gaze drifting to Matt again, now prone on his back, laughing, as her growling daughter attacked him with that monkey. A word—*restraint,* not *monkey*—Kelly needed to brand onto her brain while she still remembered the concept. And before her womb broke down altogether.

However, her womb did not call the shots. So as much as part of her might like to cradle Matt's head to her paltry bosom and make soothing, shushing noises about his needing a woman who could appreciate all that goodness and generosity, she still couldn't be that woman.

No, really.

Turning her back on the hilarity, she carefully extracted a single strand of angel-hair pasta from the frantically bubbling water, blowing on it before sucking it into her mouth.

"Ready?" Matt said behind her, scaring the bejeebers out of her.

"Mmm-hmm," she said, nodding and inhaling his scent in the tiny, steam-riddled kitchen. Reveling, maybe.

"No, let me," he said, grabbing the potholders from her hands to lug the pasta pot off the stove and over to the colander already in the sink, a move that brought solid, yummy-smelling male into contact with not-so-solid female. Yeah, that *restraint* was evaporating faster than the steam rising up from the warm, limp pasta snuggled together all cozy-like in the colander.

Kelly stared at it, thinking, *I am one sick puppy.*

All through dinner, Matt couldn't decide who was giving off weirder vibes, Coop or Kelly. One minute, the boy refused to look at Matt, the next he was staring at him like he wanted to climb into his brain. But as unsettling as that was, far stranger was Kelly's hyper, nonstop chatter. Like if Matt said "boo" she'd explode into a million pieces.

Not that, in theory, he wouldn't mind witnessing such an explosion, but at the dinner table—with the kids, anyway—wasn't what he had in mind.

And, yes, he was well aware their little do-si-do in the kitchen had brought this on. Amusing, since—God's honest truth—he'd only intended to drain the pasta. Help Kelly out like he would his mom, who'd always struggled with the spaghetti pot when it was full. Although he'd forgotten exactly how small that kitchen was.

Smiling at something Aislin said, Matt took another bite, resisting the temptation to nudge Kelly's foot under the table just to see her jump. But again. Kids.

Even so, even if they'd been alone, even though she'd become outraged on his behalf about Marcia's infidelity, and had taken his hand in the park, and invited him to dinner again, he knew she was only being kind. That she probably felt bad for him after what he'd told her.

Although to be honest he'd been horrified when he realized, a little later, that he'd probably sounded like he was playing the pity card. God knows, men did. Some men, anyway. And for some men, it worked. But Matt would stab himself in the eye before resorting to such a lame tactic.

Especially with someone he actually cared about. And he did care about Kelly. More than he probably should, more than she might ever know. However, never again would he push, or manipulate, or try to be someone he wasn't just to "get" the girl. Because he'd rather live out the rest of his life alone than in a relationship based on dishonesty.

So they'd finish dinner, and he'd offer to clean, and to read to the kidlet if she wanted, and then he'd leave. No harm, no foul, nobody making a fool out of himself.

A half hour later, he'd almost finished wiping down the counters when Kelly returned from putting the baby to bed, heaving herself up on one of the bar stools behind the breakfast bar. In some ways, she reminded him of that first night in his dad's kitchen—hair a mess, exhaustion pulling at the corners of her mouth. But the fear that had screamed in her eyes that night was gone.

Or at least changed. Although into something he couldn't have defined if his life had depended on it.

"Where's Coop?" he asked.

"Taking a bath. Under duress, believe me."

"Yeah, little boys and water are not a match made in heaven."

"Unless the water is coming out of the sky and the little boy is on a bike."

"He likes to ride in the rain?"

"He *would* like to ride in the rain. Not gonna happen. Shoot, I have enough trouble letting him ride in the dry."

"So I've noticed—"

A shrill toddler cry shunted down the hall. Sighing, Kelly pushed herself off the stool. "Linnie sometimes gets night terrors as she's falling asleep. Be back in a few…."

A minute or so later, the shrieks dulled to broken whimpers. Matt squeezed out the sponge and stuck it in the dishwasher to clean with the dishes, only to nearly have a heart attack when he turned to find a dripping little boy in a sloppily draped towel standing in the kitchen entry.

"Thought you were in the bathtub?"

"The water got cold." Shivering, and slightly squinting, Coop lifted a corner of the towel to scrub his ear. "Where's Mom?"

"With your sister." Matt stuffed his hands in his pockets. "Where's your glasses?"

"In my room. Or maybe the bathroom. I only need 'em to see important stuff, like at school." He squinted. "Or when I'm on my bike."

Matt smiled. "Need help?"

Another squint, then he said, "M-mom forgot to put pajamas in the bathroom with me. I think they're in the d-dryer—she was washing clothes earlier." More shivering. "And I d-don't like going in there."

There being the utility area of the basement, Matt assumed, where the furnace, hot-water heater and washer and dryer lived. As basements went, it really wasn't that creepy, if bare-bones. But probably not someplace a little kid wanted to be at night.

"Okay, come here…." Matt steered the child into the living room, rearranged the towel so he was actually covered then left long enough to dig spaceship-bedecked flannel pajamas, as well as a pair of SpongeBob underpants, out of the dryer.

When he returned, Coop had somehow gotten on the sofa without dislodging the towel, where he sat with his legs stretched out, squinting at his wiggling, shriveled toes. Spotting Matt, he scootched forward, grunting, until he was standing, snatched the items from Matt's hands with a muttered "Thanks" then penguin walked—the towel might've been a little tight—back to the bathroom. A minute later he emerged, glasses on, duly jammied and mostly dry, scrubbing his still-damp curls with a hand towel.

"Need anything else?" Matt said, grabbing his coat off a nearby chair.

"So do you like my mom or what?"

He might have reeled. "What—"

"You were holding her hand. In the park."

Okay, technically, Kelly had been holding Matt's hand, but… "Friends sometimes hold hands."

This time the squint wasn't because the kid *didn't* see.

"Sooo…you're Mom's friend?"

He half expected to see air quotes around *friend.*

"I'd like to think so."

"Huh."

Kid looked so serious, so…beleaguered, that all Matt wanted was to give him a hug. To reassure him that everything would be okay, even if nobody knew yet what "okay" was going to look like. But he knew little boys could be uneasy with hugging—he sure as hell had been—so instead he sat on the wooden coffee table in front of the sofa, meeting Coop's wary gaze.

"Yes, I like your mom. Same way I like you guys. It's nice, hanging out with you. All of you. And I know things probably still feel a little…off for you right now—they do, don't they?" After a moment, the boy nodded. "New school, new town, new house—"

"And Dad," Coop said, his gaze unswerving. And unnerving.

"Yeah," Matt said, figuring if the kid could shoot

straight from the hip, so would he. "And you and I, we barely know each other. I'm, like, a total stranger to you, am I right?"

"Well…not a *total* stranger. But yeah. I don't know you. Really."

"Then you have every right to be cautious. To want to protect your mom and your sister. And yourself," he said quietly. Behind his glasses, the boy's eyes widened slightly. "But I swear to you, Coop, I'd never, ever do anything to hurt any of you."

Gaze glued to Matt's, the child apparently let that sink in before he said, "So…you and Mom…?"

"Like I said. Friends. That's all."

He twisted around to look over his shoulder, then frowned back at Matt and whispered, "Promise?"

Matt placed a palm over his thumping heart…as a shadow flickered on the wall in front of him. Kelly, no doubt, he thought with a smile, listening in. "I swear. But…"

The shadow didn't move. But something inside Matt did, as he fully admitted to himself that there was something here he wanted. Or at least would like a shot at.

"I gotta be honest, though," he said, lowering his hand and smiling into the kid's still leery expression. "Maybe I wouldn't mind being a bigger part of your lives. But…that's totally up to you guys."

"You mean that?"

"Absolutely. Whatever happens—" he stood and slipped on his jacket "—it has to be right for everybody. So. Are we good?"

A beat or two passed before the boy extended his hand, giving Matt's a surprisingly firm shake. "We're good," he said, and Matt felt his heart crack.

* * *

Cloaked in the hallway's shadow, Kelly pressed her hand to her mouth. She couldn't see them, but she'd heard every word. And those words—particularly Matt's—only further eroded that restraint she wanted *so* badly to cling to.

Eroded? Try pulverized. Because while her head kept reiterating the myriad reasons why she shouldn't fall in love with the guy, her heart was sniggering and whispering, *Too late, babycakes.*

And if that weren't enough to warrant an all-expenses-paid trip to Crazyville, her little boy's bravery, not to mention his grasp on the situation, had also done a number on her. Mothers always think of their children as their babies, for sure, but…perhaps Kelly was being a trifle overprotective?

Except Coop was still only eight. Meaning even if circumstances had stolen some of his innocence, damned if she'd let them rob him of all of it. It was not Coop's responsibility, or place, to look out for her, which he was clearly doing. Yes, cute, to a point. But also scary as hell—for both their sakes.

"Hey, guys," she said, moving into the light like an actress out of the wings, all smiles and ta-da! "Oh, good, sweetie, you're in your jammies. Thanks for getting them, Matt, I totally forgot about the laundry!"

"No problem," Matt said with an odd little smile. "Linnie okay?"

It startled her to hear him call her Linnie. Since only family did that—

"She's fine. I fell asleep, too, lying with her." As her jumbled hair undoubtedly attested. Jumbled hair that seemed to absolutely fascinate Matt. "Well. Come on,

Coop," she said, holding out one arm, pathetically batting her hair with the other. "Time you hit the hay, too."

Coop nodded, then looked at Matt. "'Night, Matt. Thanks for…getting my pj's for me."

"You're welcome."

They watched the kid tromp down the hall, accompanied by a silence thick enough to insulate the entire house. Finally Matt said, "Guess I'll be going, too. Lock up behind me."

In case her brain leaked out of her ears and she forgot?

Then he was gone, leaving behind his scent and his goodness and, oh, my God, what he'd said, about being open to…more. But that it was completely up to her. Well, them.

Except…it *wasn't* up to her to ease Matt's obvious pain, to fill the hole his ex had left in his life, his heart. No matter how much, in many ways, she wished she could. Because…

Because he deserved someone whole. Someone who could love him without worrying about losing herself in the process.

Because he wasn't the only one here determined not to repeat his mistake.

Her eyes burning, Kelly hotfooted it into the kitchen and dived into her freezer for that secret stash.

Chapter Eight

At o'dark thirty a couple days later, Kelly was divesting the dryer of her unmentionables when Matt popped downstairs, his laundry basket propped on one hip. And there she was—hair uncombed, apple plugging up mouth *and* outfitted in an ancient college sweatshirt over a pair of pajama bottoms with a hole in one knee. Charming.

Then again, after the talking-to she'd given herself the other night—not to mention the sadly empty ice cream container—the crazy street-lady look could only work in her favor, no?

"Nice," he said, grinning at her overflowing basket as his crashed to the cement floor. Clearly having no issue with crazy street ladies. Drat.

Standing at the card table/folding station, Kelly removed the apple—nothin' to be done for the hair and the ensemble—and picked up a pair of her stretch briefs, about as sexy as boxed mashed potatoes. And nearly the same color. Blah cream. “You can’t be *that* hard up.”

Chuckling, Matt started to mash his clothes into the washer. Yes, lights and darks together. Apparently his mother had missed that part of his domestic education.

“Eh, it’s what’s inside that stuff that counts. The packaging’s not that important to me.”

“I see.”

“Would it be rude to mention you’re blushing?”

“Extremely.” She paused, then decided that by her mid-thirties she could talk to a man about underwear, if she so chose. Maybe not without turning the color of a radish, but you couldn’t have everything. So she continued folding for a while until Matt tossed in what looked to be a brand-new white T-shirt with his jeans, and every anal predilection she had screamed.

“Really?”

“What?” he said, looking genuinely perplexed.

She pointed to the disaster about to unfold in the washer. “You can’t mix denim and white.”

“Watch me,” he said, and she sighed. He chuckled. “If it makes you feel better, I do know that ‘rule.’ But what can I say, I’m a rebel.”

“A rebel in a baby-blue T-shirt. Fetching.”

“Actually, they usually come out sorta gray, which is fine with me.” At her obviously horrified expression, he shrugged. “Since nobody’s ever gonna see it but me, I don’t care.” He tossed in more clothes. Including a red… something. Boxers, maybe? “So neither should you, sweet cheeks.”

And this was her life, ladies and gents: a bizarre flirtation—if that was what this was—over boxers and briefs beside a belching boiler in a Jersey basement.

She picked up her apple again, chomped off a chunk.

"So," she said, chewing—because, really, could this exchange get any screwier? "Did you buy lingerie for your ex?"

"Once." He poured in detergent without measuring. No fabric softener. Punched on the machine. Leaned his butt against it with his arms crossed over his flannel shirt, clearly in no hurry to leave. "She said she had 'very particular tastes.' So she returned it for something she liked better." He snorted. "Which sums up our relationship, actually."

"Honestly, Matt!" Kelly didn't even try to keep the exasperation out of her voice. "Why on earth did she marry you? Or you, her, for that matter."

His gaze darkened. "I have no idea why she married me. Unless she thought she could make me over or something. Some women are like that, don't ask me why. Men aren't houses, for God's sake, you can't rearrange their brains like a bunch of rooms. But obviously she saw me that way. As for why I married her… She did change. Into, I suppose, who she really was. I mean, obviously we got along okay at the beginning. Had fun. And I thought we were on the same page, wanted the same things." His mouth pulled flat. "Like kids, for instance."

"She didn't want to be a mom?"

"Apparently not. And that's her choice, absolutely. But it would've been nice if she'd told me that before we got married, you know?"

Ya think? was what Kelly wanted to say, but she took another bite of the apple instead, and mumbled, "How many children did you want."

"Fifteen," Matt said, deadpan, and Kelly coughed, shaking her head when Matt went to thump her on the back. Assured she'd live, he said, "I never thought of a number, really. But we always had a full house when I was growing up." His mouth curved. "Which you know."

Recovered, Kelly smiled back. "Since I was part of it, yeah."

"Well, I liked it. Having all those people around." He paused, then shrugged. "Miss it, too."

It was the matter-of-factness of his words, the simple honesty, that made Kelly jerk her gaze away to dump out a slew of Aislin's stuff from a second basket, start folding like mad. As if that would keep his loneliness from infecting her. Right.

One of her cotton nightgowns had gotten mixed in with the load. Long. Soft. A delicate print, sprigs of violets on white. Downright virginal.

"That's pretty," Matt said. "No, really. It looks like, well… You."

She held it up, her forehead pinched. "What it looks like is something a mother wears when her kids tend to crawl in bed with her during the night."

"Which is why it looks like you."

Half smiling, she quickly folded the gown and laid it on top of Aislin's clothes. Heard herself say, "Rick bought me all kinds of sexy stuff in the beginning. Actually, well past the beginning."

"Did you wear it?"

"Of course. It made him happy. And when he was happy, I was, too."

"You can't be serious."

The combination of confusion and anger in Matt's voice made her smile. "I did eventually figure out how nuts that was." She picked up a pair of little blue jeans with embroidered flowers on the pockets, spent more time folding them than necessary. "But I'm not a lace-and-satin kind of gal. Never have been. I know that stuff makes a lot of women feel…desirable. Pretty. But oddly, it had the opposite effect on me."

"I imagine so," Matt said, still obviously pissed. "If you felt like you were pretending."

Kelly gave a miniature hot pink hoodie a sharp shake, pressed it to her chest. "Good call. But even worse…it made me feel invisible. This was about something other than, um, fantasies. Having a little *mutual* fun. This was…"

A rogue tear surprised her, trickled down her cheek. Stiffly, she quickly folded two, three, four items. "Apparently it was the *stuff* that turned Rick on. Not me." At his silence, she shouldered away the tear, then lifted her face, almost flinching at his expression. "No comment?"

"Yeah," he said, coming closer. "This…"

And then his warm hands slid around her neck and through her tangled hair—which, at his touch, was probably standing on end—and before she could say, "I haven't brushed my teeth! Or showered!" his mouth was on hers. Not that he apparently cared. And it wasn't fair because he clearly had done both, and she'd only come in here to get her clothes out of the dryer, for heaven's sake, and oh, dear *God* his mouth was soft, and warm, and wonderful, and could he tell she wasn't wearing a bra…?

"You're thinking too much," he murmured, and she reared back.

"Please don't tell me you read minds, too."

One eyebrow lifted. At least, she thought it did; he was still really, really close. As in, pelvises touching. And all the double-chocolate-chunk ice cream in the world wasn't gonna compensate for this, nope.

"Too?"

"Yeah. Too. Because you're great with the kids—" *and you kiss like an angel, if angels kissed* "—and you're patient—"

He smiled. "Not *that* patient."

"—and you're kind, and…and, well. A lot of things that aren't good." His hands had slipped around her waist. And underneath her sweatshirt. Just a hair. Just enough. Oh, hell, she thought, her forehead dropping to his chest. His lovely, solid, so-good-smelling-she-wanted-to-eat-him-up chest. "Because they are. Because *you* are."

"Haven't had our coffee yet, have we?"

"How could you tell?" Her face flushed again. "Aside from, um…" She covered her mouth.

And he uncovered it and kissed her again. Lightly. Smiling. Like this was the best morning of his life.

Not that it didn't rank right up for her, too. But she had to ask…

"Why?"

"Because…you're you," he said simply, holding her, making her feel safe, and her heart melted. Among other things. "Because you say what's on your mind—" *not everything, buddy...not even close* "—like you're not even a woman at all."

"I'm going to assume that's a compliment."

"Hell, yeah. Even so… I wasn't going to do that."

"Do what?"

His hand traveled up her back, making nice. "Make the first move. Because I'd promised myself that—if there was ever a *that*—was up to you."

Right. She knew that. Although he didn't know she knew that. So all she managed to say was "Huh." Because, no coffee. Also, screaming hormones—

"But I couldn't help it, I had to let you know… Well. You know."

"Mo-om!"

With a backward spring worthy of an high diver, Kelly jettisoned from the make-believe that was Matt and her getting cozy in the laundry room and back to her single-mom, two-kids, no-time-for-shenanigans reality.

"Be right there, just getting stuff out of the laundry!"

A slight smile flickered across Matt's mouth before he briefly touched Kelly's cheek, then started up the stairs.

Whistling.

Whew, close, Kelly thought, stacking the baskets and lugging them back to her apartment. Where, from his perch on one of the bar stools, Coop frowned at her. "Mom? Why are you smiling like that?"

Oops.

Fortunately, over the next couple insanely busy days, Kelly's hormones settled back into their accustomed coma and she could see the madness that had transpired in the laundry room for the folly it was. True, as follies went, kisses ranked pretty low on the scale—she wasn't fourteen, for crying out loud. But there were kisses that really were only kisses, and kisses that winked and said, "This is only a hint, baby."

A hint of things she had a strong feeling would be nothing like things she'd experienced before. Meaning maybe her hormones weren't quite as comatose as they'd have her believe.

Little rotters.

The oven timer beeped. Hauling herself out of la-la land, Kelly extracted a couple test pans of hors d'oeuvres she was thinking about serving for the Thomases' anniversary party the following night, and slammed shut the oven door with her hip. Cheese bubbled and shrimp sizzled, making her smile. *Lookin' good,* she thought, laying the pans on racks on the counter. Since this party was at the couple's house—a million-dollar number in the chichi part of town—she'd do most of the actual cooking on-site, anyway, so testing it in her certified kitchen wasn't a priority. And, anyway, the new range Matt had installed wasn't exactly shabby. High-end, no, but definitely a solid, reliable product.

Just like Matt.

Jeez, Louise…

A thousand times she'd told herself she would not pick up the gauntlet he had thrown down. Or even look at it. Or think about it, sitting there. Taunting. Only then she'd remember his touch, that kiss, so sweet it made her girl parts sigh—yes, still—and she'd find herself taking the *tiniest* peek to see if the gauntlet was still there.

Like where was it going to go…?

Out front, she heard a car pull up behind her van in the driveway. The windows were set too high to see—annoying, that—but a second later her phone rang.

"I'm here," her mother-in-law said. "Do I use the front door?"

"No, follow the path around to your left."

Seconds later Lynn bustled inside, tucking her leather driving gloves in her hobo bag. Only woman Kelly knew who could make mom jeans and ballet flats look chic. "I know, I know, I'm early. Hope that's not a problem?"

"Of course not," Kelly said, giving her a hug. "Although Linnie's asleep and Coop's not out of school for another hour—"

"Oh, my God, what smells so good?"

Smiling, Kelly took the purse, as well as Lynn's heavy cardigan, and set them on a nearby chair. "Test runs for tomorrow's shindig. They're in the kitchen, help yourself. Although they're right out of the oven, so still hot—"

"Hot is good," Lynn said, making a beeline for the tiny kitchen, delicately piling an assortment on a napkin plucked from the holder on the breakfast bar.

"There's coffee, too," Kelly said. "Mugs are in the cupboard over the maker."

"Great."

A moment later, amidst a gasp or two as she tried chewing the morsels before they'd cooled, Lynn returned to the living room, napkin in one hand, mug in the other, her eagle eyes missing nothing.

"When you said 'basement apartment,' I have to admit, I was skeptical. Because I think of that god-awful place Jack and I had off Second Avenue in lower Manhattan, when we were first married. Casa Cucaracha." She shuddered. "But this is lovely, really. So much light! And the colors you've used—like those shows on TV. And these—" she hoisted the appetizer-laden napkin, rolled her eyes "—fantastic. Whatever these people are paying you, it's not enough—"

"What's going on, Lynn?" Kelly said, sitting on the arm of the chair where she'd put her mother-in-law's things. Because not only was Lynn never early for anything, the praisefest was also a little much. Even for her.

Lynn's gaze wrestled with Kelly's for a moment before she released a sigh, then lowered herself to the edge of the sofa, setting her goodies on the coffee table. "Smart, too," she said on a short laugh, then folded her hands on her lap. "Did Coop mention our phone conversation the other evening?"

Kelly snorted. "As if. Very private person, our Coop. Then again, since I knew it was you, I figured it was okay to give him his space."

Lynn glanced around as though the child might materialize out of thin air. "And you're sure he won't be home yet?"

"Since he can't get here unless I pick him up, very. Lynn…?"

Sighing, she fluffed her bangs, then toyed with a gold

bangle on her wrist. "Okay." Another sigh. "He told me about you and Matt holding hands. When you were at the park."

"What? Oh. Crap."

"Now, you don't have to explain anything to *me*—"

"Yes, I do. Because it wasn't that kind of holding hands. Matt had told me something about his ex that ticked me off, that she'd *cheated* on him, and I felt bad, so I… It was one of those I-understand kind of things, that's all. As a friend—"

"And now who's talking too much?" Lynn said, chuckling when Kelly stopped, mouth open. "Like I didn't know why you interrupted me a minute ago?"

Kelly's mouth flattened. Although what were the odds that Lynn would attribute the blush to the oven's heat? "I didn't think Coop saw—he and Aislin were twenty feet away, and we're talking ten seconds, tops—but if he'd asked me about it, I would've told him the same thing. And why on earth did he talk to you and not me?"

"Because I was a convenient sounding board would be my guess," Lynn said gently. "I doubt there's any more to it than that."

Maybe. Maybe not. "Was he…upset?"

"More…trying to process, I think. Which is why I decided to say something now."

"And as I said—"

"I know what you said. That's not the point."

"What's not the point?"

She smiled. "Whether you're telling me the whole truth or not."

"I…" Kelly frowned. "What?"

Lynn laughed again. "Sweetheart, I'm not judging. Why would I? It's like I said to Coop, I don't know. But…I saw how Matt was around you at the funeral. How he was with the children." She picked up her coffee again, her mouth twitching. "How red your face is now. Oh, for God's sake, honey… It's been more than two years. Time to move on, don't you think?"

"Lynn, I…"

"No. It's taken me nearly a week to work up to this, so now you listen." She lowered her eyes to the mug, tapping the handle with one finger, then said, "I never said anything, but when you asked Rick for a divorce…" Her gaze lifted to Kelly's. "Even though I saw what he was doing to you and the children, I was not happy about it. Because I felt like you'd given up on him. On what you'd had."

"But…I thought you said—"

"That you'd fought for your marriage, I know. This wasn't about logic, which is why I kept my trap shut. You had no choice, I get that. I got it at the time. But, see, I knew how Rick would react. And as his mother…"

Her eyes filled, bringing tears to Kelly's. "Well," Lynn said with a slight smile, "you know how that goes. However, it wasn't up to you, or me, to fix him. He was a grown man, capable of making his own choices. And you had to put the babies' welfare first, which you've always done. Are still doing—"

"Exactly. And what you don't know—" Kelly sighed "—is that I overheard a conversation between Matt and Coop, after he talked to you. Kid came right out and asked if Matt 'liked' me."

Lynn's brows lifted. "And?"

"And…after saying he did, but as a *friend,* Matt admitted he'd like to be more. To all of us."

"And was this a surprise?"

Another wave of heat washed through her. "No. *But,*" she said to Lynn's chuckle, "he also reassured Coop he was waiting for a cue from me. Not in those words, but close."

"And is he going to get that cue?"

"I'm not exactly in the position to give him one, am I?"

"Then let me rephrase that. Do you want to?"

"It's not about what I *want*—"

"And why not?"

"Because, for one thing, Coop's been through enough in the past little while, don't you think? And if you could have heard him, confronting Matt like a little bulldog hell-bent on protecting me..." She shook her head. "And even if that weren't the case—" her sigh was rough enough to hurt "—Rick made me believe he'd take care of me, a promise I ate up like candy. A promise that nearly destroyed both of us. I will never put myself, or another man, in that position again."

"So you've decided to martyr yourself to the idea of some...some idealistic idea of womanhood that doesn't need men?"

"Martyr's maybe a little strong. But after everything I went through—"

"I know what you went through. I was there, remember? And I saw this little mouse of a girl blossom into something I frankly wouldn't have thought possible even five years ago. But—and this is my point—don't confuse your newfound strength with never needing male company, if you get my drift."

Kelly barked out a laugh. "Says the woman who never married after her husband died."

"Oh, honey..." This time Lynn's laugh was rich. Full. "True. But for one thing, that doesn't mean I've ruled out the possibility. And for another..." Her eyes sparkled. "It doesn't mean I've taken the veil, either. Sweetie, I've had a lover for years."

"What?"

"You heard me. We have an...arrangement that suits us

both," she said to Kelly's obviously stunned expression. "For now, at least. And trust me, no one was more shocked that I was, when this…opportunity presented itself and I realized I was game. That I still wanted a man's companionship. A man's *touch. And* that I could have that without losing my autonomy."

"And… Wait. Nobody knew?"

"Not a living soul."

"Not even Rick?"

"Are you kidding? Especially not Rick."

"Wow. This is… Wow." Kelly squinted. "Does this man have a name?"

"Of course. But I'm not telling. Not yet. And no, before your brain runs amok, he's not married. And he's nobody you know." She chuckled. "Like I said. I have no idea what is or isn't going on between you and that sweet, hunky landlord of yours. And I do understand your need for independence. And to protect the kids, before you get on my case about *that.* But believe it or not, you can do, and be, all those things and still have a little fun. To enjoy being *wanted,*" she said with a coy little hitch of her shoulders. "Isn't it wonderful that women can write their own stories however they wish these days?"

Kelly crossed her arms. "And if I want to write mine without a hero?"

Lynn gave her an inscrutable look, then shrugged again. "If that's what your heart's telling you, then fine. Only you know what's best for you—"

"It's not only about what's best for me. Or even the kids. Because Matt…" Blinking, she glanced away, then back. "I'm simply not strong enough for another relationship."

"Oh, please… Nobody's talking caterers and wedding gowns here. What's wrong with a little fling?"

Kelly choked on her laugh. "You can't be serious."

"Why not? Did it ever occur to you that maybe you deserve *that?* And, anyway…who's to say Matt's not strong enough for both of you…?"

"Don't even go there, Lynn. Because I'm sure as hell not. Not again. Not ever."

"And if you don't, how will you ever know when you're strong enough? Huh? And look who's awake!"

With a this-isn't-over-yet glance at Kelly, Lynn set down her coffee and held her arms out to Aislin, who was standing—well, wobbling was more like it—at the end of the hallway, yawning hugely and practically strangling Stripes, the monkey. Then a big smile bloomed across the flushed little face as she ran to her grandmother and crawled into her lap.

"Oh, my goodness," Lynn said, palming Aislin's damp curls, "somebody's all sweaty from her nap!"

"Yeah, she usually is," Kelly said, thinking, *A reason to get out of here, yay.* "Hold on, let me get some fresh clothes."

Although, she mused as she trekked to Aislin's mint-and-rose room, it wasn't as if she'd left her jumbled thoughts in the living room. Or that she could change them for fresh ones like the baby's clothes. Although by the time she left to pick up Coop from school—having left her girl child in her adoring grandmother's very capable hands—most of the jumble had begun to fade enough for Lynn's last words to flash in her brain like a Times Square billboard:

And if you don't, how will you ever know when you're strong enough…?

Which was pretty much what she'd told herself the other evening, wasn't it? Except there was a big difference between feeding the man spaghetti and cookies and getting naked with him.

Shuddering, Kelly pulled into the queue of cars waiting for the bell and rolled down the window for some much needed fresh air. Not that her mother-in-law didn't have a point, but…there was another person involved here. A person who'd been badly stung, who'd clearly wanted the whole enchilada before, and Kelly highly doubted that had changed. So Matt would probably scoff at the very idea of a…fling. A word, let alone a concept, she found pretty darn scoff worthy herself, actually.

Because she was so not a fling…er.

Then she and her girl parts remembered that kiss, and she thought, *Hmm.*

The school bell rang, piercing her thoughts. Kelly propped her elbow on the steering wheel, her head nestled in her hand, as wave after wave of shrieking kidlets poured like lava toward the pick-up lane. She smiled when Coop reached the van and clambered in behind her.

"Where's Linnie?" he asked over his seat belt's comforting click.

"With Grandma. She got here early. You and Linnie are spending the weekend with her, remember?"

"Oh, yeah, huh."

Kelly waited until they'd pulled away from the school and the traffic had thinned out before she said, "So she tells me you guys had a rather intense chat the other evening. When we got home from the park?"

"Oh?" Silence. Then he asked, "What did she say?"

"That you saw Matt and me holding hands and didn't quite know what to think."

"Oh." She heard shuffling behind her. "S'okay, it's no big deal."

"That's not what Grandma thought," Kelly said carefully. No answer. "Honey…first off, anytime you see or hear something you don't understand, I'm here. You can talk to me about anything—"

"I know."

"Well, remember that. And second…you're right. It wasn't any big deal. Matt had told me something that made me feel badly for him, so I was…showing my support. That's all."

"So you don't want him to be your boyfriend?"

Oh, brother. Even over the traffic noise, she heard the worry in his voice. Heard her heartbeat thrumming in her ears. "It doesn't… I don't…" She cleared her throat, frowning at the car ahead of her. "Matt and I are just friends, sweetie."

"Yeah, that's what he said, too."

"Then there you are."

Kelly couldn't quite tell, but she thought he might have sighed. "Did you make more cookies?"

"Sorry, not today. Had to practice for my event tomorrow. But, again. Grandma. I'm sure she'll have a treat or two for you, don't you think?"

"Yeah, prob'ly."

A few minutes later, they pulled into their driveway. Once out of the car, Kelly intercepted Coop before he zoomed to the apartment, grabbing his shoulders and bending to look him in the eye. As much as she could, anyway, through end-of-the-day smudges on his lenses. "Have I told you recently how proud I am of you?"

His eyebrows pushed slightly together. "Proud? How come?"

Smiling, she smoothed back his curls, relishing this small act that would probably get axed from the "acceptable" list before much longer. "Because you're one of the bravest people I know. And trust me on this—you and Aislin absolutely come first in my life. I will never do anything without considering how it would affect you guys. Got that?"

The corners of what used to be *the* most adorable cupid mouth curved up. "Yeah."

"I love you so much, pookie."

"I love you, too, Mom. Except..." He made the "stinky face" that had cracked her up ever since he was a baby.

"Right, sorry, I forgot. But I still get to do this," Kelly said, messing with his curls, which got a heavy sigh—and a real smile, this time—before he took off for the apartment.

She straightened, feeling the chilly breeze ruffle her own hair like an angel's caress. Her gaze shot to Matt's living room window but all she saw was the sun's glare bouncing off the glass. And her disappointment was so sharp that he wasn't there, wasn't watching her, it stole her breath.

The thing was, she wasn't in denial. She knew what she wanted. Or, in this case, who. Wanted so badly, in fact, the thought of not allowing herself to have it—him—was making her crazier than she already was. It'd been two years—well, closer to two and a half years, come to think of it—since she'd had sex. And she'd honestly thought she hadn't missed it. Then again, when there's no one around you want to have sex *with,* what's to miss?

Sighing, Kelly finally followed her son inside, where Lynn, bless her heart, was happily herding her grand-babies. She'd already pulled together a bag of things for Linnie, was now directing Coop to do the same. Ten minutes later, they were gone, leaving Kelly alone with her thoughts, roughly five million hors d'oeuvres and a libido on speed.

Outside, she heard the Explorer pull into the driveway, Matt's rich laugh as Alf apparently chased a bird with the audacity to land in the front yard, and her heart went *whompa-whompa-whompa.* And she realized what she missed wasn't sex, per se. What she missed—craved—was intimacy. Connection. Being open and honest and bare—in every sense of the word—with another human being.

The kind of connection she'd finally admitted, God knows how long ago, she'd never really had with her husband, even in the early days when she'd loved him with all her heart. And which she now realized, with a breath-stealing *whoosh* of revelation—as in, damned if the room didn't suddenly seem brighter—she *deserved.*

Just like Lynn had said.

Just like she had said to Matt.

Overhead, Kelly heard Matt's muffled footfalls, the dog's galumphing. Imagined she heard him talking stupid to the dog, saw his grin. Her pulse throbbing, she looked over at all those goodies, snugly nestled in assorted plastic containers, and reminded herself—sternly—she was in charge of her own destiny. More than she'd ever been, actually. That it was up to her right now whether to indulge this new, scary, reckless side of herself or play it safe.

Except... Her entire life she'd opted for *safe,* and where had that gotten her?

Exactly nowhere, she thought, and pulled her cell phone from her pocket.

Chapter Nine

He should've known Grandma would rat him out to Mom, Cooper thought later, after Grandma had taken him and Linnie down to the duck pond near her apartment. And yeah, he was still pretty ticked about that. Although it was his own dumb fault for saying anything in the first place.

Hard as he could, he threw a piece of stale bread, and the ducks—at least twenty, maybe—zoomed across the pond like they hadn't eaten in forever. It almost felt like spring, sunny and not nearly as cold as it had been. He could even hear a robin singing somewhere. Laughing, Linnie clapped, then held out her chubby little starfish hand.

"My turn!"

Must be nice, being too little to really understand what was going on. Or care, anyway. Coop handed over a piece of bread and Linnie took off toward the water, calling to the ducks.

"Linnie, stop!" he yelled. "You'll fall in!"

She turned, her mouth pushed down at the corners. "But I can't throw that far! The ducks won't get it!"

"Look!" Grandma said, pointing and laughing.

The baby whipped around, then let out a shriek. Because the ducks had climbed out of the pond and were waddling right toward her, quacking like crazy.

"No, ducks! *No!*" She backed away, holding the bread over her head as the ducks crowded her, quacking louder and louder. "Go *away!* Coop! Help! They're gonna eat me!"

"No, they're not, honey," Grandma said, still laughing. "Cooper, go help your sister."

Ducks streaked every which way as he ran over, then picked her up, grunting. Man, she was getting big. Almost too big for him to hold, which made him a little sad. Then he had this sort of foggy memory, of being in Dad's arms. When he was little, before everything got all messed up. At the zoo, maybe? He couldn't remember. But the back of his throat got real scratchy.

"It's okay," he said, swallowing. "Just rip the bread in little chunks and throw it to them."

After a moment, Aislin started pinching off itty-bitty pieces and dropping them one by one on the ground, giggling when the noisy ducks bunched around them, their pointy little tails twitching. Then she suddenly said, "Daddy's dead, huh?" and Coop nearly dropped her.

"Yeah. He is." He hiked her up in his arms, frowning at the side of her face. "Do you know what that means?"

"Mama said it means he's someplace we can't see him," she said, pinching off another piece of bread. "And that he's not coming back. Because he can't." She got quiet for a moment, then pointed to a duck with a green head, all shimmery in the sun. "He's pretty. Can I get down now?"

"You sure?"

"You won't let them hurt me?"

Coop had no idea how little kids' brains worked, but was it strange that Linnie seemed more worried about the ducks than Dad being dead? Then again, maybe it was better that way. "'Course not," he said. "Anyway, they're only ducks."

"I *know* that," she said, all huffy—like she hadn't screamed for him to come save her five seconds ago—then squirmed out of his arms to finish feeding them her slice of bread. Then Coop felt Grandma's arm slip around his shoulders.

"Your dad would be so proud of you," she said, and now the scratchy feeling turned into a pinchy one, only this time inside his chest. For a moment, he wanted to tell Grandma—heck, to tell somebody, anybody—what he was feeling. Except how could he? Because everybody had enough to worry about without him making things worse, right?

So Coop sorta smiled up at Grandma, then walked down to the water, where nobody could see how hard he was trying not to cry. Because even though his life wasn't bad anymore, he wanted things to be better. No, more than better. *Good.* Like, happy good. Even if he wasn't sure what that was supposed to be.

Although, apparently, neither did the grown-ups.

Which was the saddest thing of all.

Matt had no idea—when Kelly called an hour ago to say she'd made way too many appetizers, would he like to share?—why he'd suggested she bring them to his place. Okay, that wasn't entirely true, he wanted her to come *here* because he wanted her in *his* bed. On the *very* off chance that was how the evening played out.

Of course, if it didn't, that was okay, too. Still, he could have sworn he'd heard a *maybe* in her voice. Or, more likely, in his own head.

But really, he was cool with whatever happened.

Or didn't.

Then he'd looked around his apartment and realized that, fixed up though the place now was, it definitely looked like a bachelor lived here. Not that Matt was slovenly—all rooms with plumbing met his mother's standards, mostly, and he didn't dare leave out takeout boxes or the dog would have a field day—but aside from that, the decor ran to dust bunnies and fur. And while he regularly did his laundry, actually putting it away was not high on his list.

And he'd had to change his sheets.

Also, make a run to the drugstore. Since he didn't exactly have a condom dispenser in his bedroom.

So his heart was racing from *his* racing when he—and Alf—answered the doorbell…until his brain registered what his eyes saw and that heart took a pratfall.

"Wow," he said, grateful to get that much out, as the dog, sensing food, obediently sat, and Kelly blushed. And it wasn't like she looked ready for the red carpet or anything, but compared with her usual wild-haired, makeupless, slightly frazzled look, this was…

Wow.

Yeah, she was wearing jeans, but these fit. Like, *really* fit. And over them, a sorta frilly white top that hinted at cleavage. And over that, a soft, floaty, light green sweater that reminded him of spring. As in soft breezes and sunshine and lying in the grass and looking up at the clouds. And kissing. He also had no idea what she'd done to her hair, but the curls actually glittered in the pot lights' soft glow. She'd darkened her lashes, too. And put on lip stuff.

Huh. Maybe *maybe* was looking more promising?

Matt took the plastic-wrapped tray of finger food, stood

aside to let her in. Got a whiff of something delicate. Floral. Hopeful.

"You smell good," he said, and she laughed.

"Kids were gone, I decided to take a bubble bath."

"Sounds like fun."

"What it was was glorious. A gift from Lynn ages ago, first chance I've had to use it. And I really like that wall color."

"Um…thanks."

Alf sticking close—to fend off any random marauding hordes, most likely—Matt carted the tray to the dining table, setting it beside the bottle of wine he'd scored while he was out getting the, um, other things. A move that at least gave him a chance to breathe.

"Wasn't sure what you were bringing," he said, uncorking the wine, "so I hope red's okay…?"

"What? Oh. Sure. Red's fine."

Bottle in hand, he turned. Caught Kelly staring really hard at a framed watercolor Ethan's oldest had done when she was six—which looked exactly like you'd expect a first-grader's painting to look—as she twirled a curl around her index finger. Hell, he could practically hear her heartbeat from here.

And he sighed.

"Hey." Frozen in midtwist, she met his gaze. "What's going on?" he asked softly.

"What makes you think…?"

"You're wearing lipstick," he said, and she snorted. Only to drop onto his leather sofa, hand extended.

"Wine. Now."

Matt poured half a glass, carried it to her. Watched, bemused, as she sucked it down in three gulps. "You don't normally drink, do you?"

She shook her head. Then, on a soft "Whoa," shut her

eyes. "And this is why, because I've got the alcohol tolerance of a gnat." Eyes still closed, she sighed. "But then, I don't normally do this, either."

"Come on to your landlord?"

"You're really enjoying this, aren't you?"

"Only if that's what you're really doing." When Kelly snorted again, Matt pried the glass from her stranglehold, carried it back to the table. "But I'm cutting you off."

One eye opened. "And why would you do that?"

"Because I'd kinda like you to enjoy this, too."

"Oh." Then she covered her face with her hands and mumbled, "I have no idea what I'm doing."

Matt sat beside her, tugged her hands away. Offered the plate. "Eat."

"I'm not—"

"You're swaying. Eat."

"Am not…." She dropped her hands, only to grab the sofa arm. "Okay, maybe a little."

He waited until she made her selection—although since she wasn't looking at the plate, *selecting* was pushing it—then chose one for himself. Chicken in some puffy biscuit…thing. With a kick to it that surprised him. After a minute or so of silent munching—on both their parts—Matt sat forward to sip from his own glass, then asked, very softly, "Why?"

There was a weighty pause, then she said, "Because the alternative sucked?"

He looked at her over his shoulder. "The alternative being…?"

"Letting fear keep making choices for me."

Matt offered one of the appetizers to the dog, who delicately took it, giving him a strange look before carrying it to the other end of the room, where he'd undoubtedly find the mangled remains the next day. Then he reached for Kelly's hand, holding it between both of his. Yep, cold as ice. "But you're still scared."

Her sharp laugh pinged around the room. "You might say."

Gently chafing her frigid hands in his own, Matt asked, "Got any idea why?"

"Because it's been more than two years since I've had sex? Because my husband was my one and only…?"

"You're kidding?"

That got a sharp look. "Yes, Matt, I was a virgin until the ripe old age of twenty-one. Is this a problem?"

Matt shook his head. "Nope—"

"And I don't want to hurt you."

His brows flew up. "Me? What on earth…?"

"I can't promise anything past…" Her eyes got all watery. "Past right now."

"And I don't expect you to," he said gently, thinking *Damn.* Because, you know. Hope.

He strangled a sigh. "Honey, people…mess around all the time without a commitment—"

"People, yes," Kelly said, popping up. "Me, no. Which you yourself pointed out, if you recall. So all this feels—" she made a circling motion with her hand "—slightly… wobbly."

Matt stood, as well. "I'm thinking that's the wine."

Hugging herself, she gave a hiccupy kind of laugh. And a voice said, *For God's sake, do something!* So he tugged her close, and she sniffed a little, and sighed.

She threaded her arms around his waist and hugged him back and whispered, "You deserve so much more than I can give."

"And if I'm okay with that?" he heard himself say, and she reared back to look into his eyes.

"You're sure? I mean, absolutely, positively sure? Because—"

"Of what I said to Coop? Yes, I knew you were there listening."

On a sigh, she pressed her forehead to his chest again and nodded, her hair tickling his chin.

He lifted her head again to cup her jaw in both hands, watching her pulse tick at the base of her throat. "The whole reason I said what I did to Coop is because I care about you. All of you, sure. But especially you." He paused. "Same as ever. So if you're having second thoughts, that's okay. I'll be extremely disappointed—" that got a little smile "—but it's entirely your call."

"Why?" she said, her eyes searching his. "Why me?"

The same question she'd asked before, he realized. The same disbelieving look in her eyes, which pissed him off. "Because you're brave and funny and sexy even when you look like crap—" a startled laugh burst out of her throat "—and most of all, because you're a straight shooter. And that's the thing, see—as long as you're honest with me, I'm good. Whatever happens, or doesn't…don't pretend."

After a moment, a small smile curved her mouth. "I'd never do that to you, Matt. I promise."

"Then I don't see a problem."

"Yeah, well, I do," she said, and his heart sank…until he realized she was yanking his shirttail out of his jeans. And that her glasses were…somewhere else. "Because we're both wearing way too many clothes." She laughed. Nervously. "And you should see your face right now…."

A breath later Matt plunged his hands through all those magnificent curls and claimed her mouth, and she melted, making little purring sounds in her throat, and he sank into a kiss so wet and deep and crazy he never wanted to find his way out.

But he did—somehow—and backed up to smile into that beautiful, bewildered, unfocused gaze.

"One more promise," he said, and she looked like she might smack him. "Whatever baggage either of us has? Goes no further than the bedroom door."

"Done," she said, and he literally swept her off her feet, just to hear her laugh.

Okay, so she might have been a trifle overconfident about ditching the baggage, Kelly thought as Matt kicked shut the bedroom door—

"Dog sleeps on the bed with me, could get awkward."

Or at least, *all* the baggage—

Light went on by the bed. *Not doing this in the dark. Got it.*

Because, the heat and tingles and gasps aside, Matt would be only the second man to see her naked. To touch her where only one other man had touched. Slightly terrifying prospect, that. Exhilarating, yes. But terrifying.

He tugged her to sit beside him on the already turned-down bed. Tans and browns, all male. And smelling of Tide, she thought, smiling—

"You're doing it again," he whispered, scraping his whiskered chin along—oh!—her jawline as he rolled her cardigan off her shoulders, down her arms…

"Doing wh-what?"

His mouth—warm, soft, talented—worked down her neck. Her eyes may have crossed. "Thinking," he mumbled. "Stop it."

As if. "Okay."

His laugh was more of a rumble. "I'm serious. Lift your arms. Or…not," he said to her frown. "If I'm rushing things…"

"No! It's not that. It's…" Kelly huffed a sigh. "It's…"

Oh, hell. She crossed her arms. "You don't get to call all the shots, okay?"

"Hey. As long as shots get called, does it really matter who calls 'em?" At her frown, he said, "Okay…how's about we trade off every so often? You, then me, then you again. Sound good?"

"And how's that supposed to work, exactly?"

His eyes darkened. And not with lust. Not *only* with lust, anyway. Slowly, softly, he swept her hair away from her shoulder. "Somehow, between the two of us, I think we can figure it out."

Somehow, she figured he was probably right. A second later, she whisked the silk top over her head, shivering at the static crackling along her skin, in her hair—

Her skin sizzled at his stare. Honestly, she felt like the most inexperienced goober in New Jersey. Then, grinning, he met her gaze. "Kinda hard to demonstrate my skill at removing a bra one-handed if you're not wearing one."

"Seemed…superfluous," she said, and he chuckled. "You really couldn't tell? Before?"

Matt shrugged. And stared some more. And yet the more he stared, the less exposed she felt. If anything, she felt…sheltered. "Thought maybe it was one of those not-really-there numbers. Lace or something."

"I don't do lace, remember?"

"Oh, right. Forgot."

Then, in one muscle-rippling move, his own shirt was gone, and…oh, my, yes. And then some. Then, smiling, he laid her back on the bed as he kissed her again, and again, and again and again, not touching her breasts, each kiss deeper, longer than the one before it, and she felt everything…melting…yielding…except for her nipples, which by this time were *begging.* For his hands, his mouth, anything but all this stupid *air* between them—

A laugh bubbled from her throat between those kisses, those wicked, wonderful kisses that had traded the terror for *yesyesyesohplease*....

"What?" Matt said, smiling against her mouth.

"Oh, you're good."

"Oh, just wait," he said, and she smacked him. Then grabbed his shoulders. All granitey and such, they were.

"Touch me."

"Not yet."

"Are you *kidding* me?"

"Hey. It's my turn, right?"

Like she knew anymore. "Except you're not doing anything!"

More grinning. His slightly rough fingertip traced her jawline, trailed to the hollow of her throat...and she gasped. And—oh, hell—whimpered.

"Not doing a damn thing, nope."

"You are so dead."

Now his breath was warm in her ear. "Patience, pumpkin," he said, and kissed her some more, then grinned into her eyes. "It's not every day a guy gets to live out his teenage fantasy."

Took her a moment. "Oh. Really?"

"Really. Of course, there were others. Fantasies, I mean. As we got older. But when I was thirteen... Yeah." He slowly swept one fingertip across her bottom lip. "These made me crazy."

"Not..." She glanced down at her breasts.

"That didn't happen until later."

"Since neither did they, you mean."

"Something like that, yeah. They're very pretty, by the way." At her eye roll, he chuckled, then leaned back, head propped in his hand. She really was gonna kill him. Until she noticed his gaze had darkened again, that the smile had vanished. "This, right now—it really is all about you. What *you* want." He shifted again to cup her face. "What you *want*."

Suddenly self-conscious, Kelly sat up, grabbing a pillow to cover herself. "But what about you? What do *you* want?"

The smile returned. Less teasing, more…something. A something that made her shudder with equal parts anticipation and apprehension that whatever was about to happen wouldn't leave her where it found her. "What I've got right now," he whispered, then sat forward to cradle her skull in his palm and kiss her again. And maybe she wasn't the most experienced chick-a-doodle on the planet, but if that was a kiss about *now,* she'd eat Linnie's stuffed monkey.

Because there was promise in that kiss, by gum… promise, too, when he gently tugged the pillow away, laid her down and, at long, long last, touched her breasts…at first the barest whisper of knuckle across first one nipple, then the other as he kissed her…then moved to her jaw…her throat…her collarbone…and when his lips *finally* closed around her nipple, she sighed and smiled and wrapped her arms around his neck, her hand in his short, bristly hair, and simply…*let.* Let him have at it, at her, let herself live in this incredibly precious moment.

Then, on another evil chuckle, Matt pressed his mouth to her belly, unzipping her jeans inch by inch…and it was magic and heaven and Christmas all rolled into one, what he was doing, how he was making her feel…how she was letting *herself* feel, cherished, and confident, and so, so alive.

And tears leaked from her eyes, of joy, and amazement, and maybe even a little gratitude.

Then he tugged off her jeans and panties, both at once—so skilled, he was—and spread her legs, and kissed her *there*, and she thought, *yes*, and *oh, please*, and then she said the words out loud because she wanted him to know she *wanted* him, she wanted *him,* and somewhere in there she might have mentioned the condoms in her purse, and he chuckled and said, "Got it covered," which was when she realized he was naked, too. Except for one crucial part which was thankfully not.

So she opened to him even more, inviting, but he whispered, "Not yet."

"No, you don't understand," she said, tense, expectant, and he said, "Oh, trust me, I do," and then it was only about his mouth, and the joy—oh! the *joy!*—liquid and tingling and sparkling, and her cries as she tumbled over the edge and straight to Nirvana. And she thought—eyes shut, grinning, panting—*now I get it.*

Also, hallelujah.

Then he pushed her knees apart, and her eyes popped open.

"Seriously?" she said.

And he smiled and said, "Trust me," and slid inside her, filling her, but not enough, not like she needed to be filled—

"More," she whispered, lifting her hips, and he shifted, cupping her bottom, and…

Yes, there, like that....

"Good?"

"Mmm-hmm…"

Then he stilled, trembling slightly, and Kelly opened her eyes to see him looking at her like she was a miracle, and suddenly she was mad that Rick had never looked at her at all when they'd had sex, much less as though she was a miracle, that he'd never bothered to make sure it was as good for her as it was for him. Then she got madder still at herself for accepting that, for never saying, "Hey, buster! You're not the only one in this bed—!"

"You okay?" Matt whispered, stroking a thumb across her temple.

"Yes. Why?"

"You're frowning."

She pulled him closer, letting herself sink so deeply into his gaze she knew there'd be no turning back. "Not for long, I imagine," she said.

And let go.

The sky was still that blah, not-quite-daylight color when Matt bolted upright, annoyance spiking when he realized he was alone. He crashed back onto his pillow, breathing hard, telling himself this wasn't a surprise, that he should just shut up and be thankful for what they'd shared—

Wait. Where was the dog? And was that…bacon?

Happiness glimmered.

Because unless Alf had learned how to cook in the past twelve hours, the woman who'd rocked his world last night—more than once—was making breakfast.

And maybe she's just hungry.

There was that.

Still, with a joint-popping stretch he got out of bed, tended to business, pulled on jeans and a sweatshirt. By now the scents of coffee and cinnamon mingled with the bacon, tugging him to the kitchen—sunny, eat-in, outdated—where Kelly, her back to the door, chatted away to Alf as she cooked. She'd apparently gone back to her apartment to change, her curls blazing against the dull gray of that baggy, god-awful Seton Hall hoodie. Could've fit two of her in there, he mused, but knowing—really knowing, not guessing anymore—what was underneath the hoodie? Yow.

Softly smiling, Matt linked his arms over his growling stomach and leaned against the doorjamb, watching her.

Being a dude, he was no stranger to the concept of sex and love being two distinct things. Heaven knew, before his marriage, he'd had some pretty enjoyable encounters along the way with no emotional attachment whatsoever. Not a lot, maybe, but enough to know what he was talking about. Hell, even he and Marcia had fooled around up to the end—her ploy, he now knew, to keep him from guessing about her secret life—and it had been well past the expiration date on any real feelings between them. If there ever had been, he thought sourly. So love was definitely not a prerequisite for good sex.

But he was beginning to think it might be for *great* sex. As in, potentially life altering. Sure, he'd known he had feelings for Kelly, but…

Yeah. Stuff just got real.

For him, anyway.

The dog finally wrenched her attention from the bacon strips lying on a paper towel on the old gas stove to give him a good-morning bark, and Kelly whipped around.

"Hey," she said, with an almost shy smile, and Matt instantly covered the few feet between them to haul her against his chest, lay one on her. Which she returned, absolutely, but still, when they broke apart he saw a whole bunch of questions in her eyes. God knew women were no picnic to figure out under ordinary circumstances, but this one was the biggest tangle of contradictions he'd ever known.

"What?" he said, and she smiled. And blushed.

"I can't stop thinking about last night."

Sex talk, bacon *and* blushing? Best. Morning. Ever. He tugged her closer. "Oh, yeah?"

"Yeah." More blushing. Adorable. And hot. "I kinda broke some new ground, there. Once or twice."

Huh. True, way, *way* in the back of his mind he thought maybe she'd seemed a little surprised now and then. But while he wasn't into the kinky stuff, he did know about it. And what they'd done didn't even come close.

"You should've said, if something didn't feel right."

Her laugh startled him. She linked her hands around his neck, her smile fading slightly. "You have no idea," she said softly, "how right things felt. Besides, do you think I'd still be here if they hadn't?"

Okay. He could work with that. He reached around her to snag a piece of bacon. She'd cooked up an entire package, looked like. Which she sure as hell hadn't found in his fridge. "But you didn't have to make breakfast."

"For you, maybe not. For me, yes. I woke up starving."

Matt chomped off a bite of the bacon, ignoring his drooling dog. Not to mention the impulse to point out that since she'd obviously gone downstairs to change clothes and get the bacon, she could've stayed there, fed her starving self in her own kitchen. So…yeah.

"Whatever works," he said, giving her a quick kiss on the lips. "I'm just grateful."

"Oh, wait…" Kelly slipped out of his arms to open the oven door, flooding the room with warmth and even more amazing smells. The dog whimpered. Matt relented and fed her the last bite of his bacon. "One's a scrambled-egg casserole with cheese and scallions," she said, "the other's baked French toast."

"Wow." And he'd thought the *sex* had been fantastic. "I usually make do with Wheaties."

Snorting, she grabbed a pair of pot holders to pull first one, then the other, baking dish from the oven, plunking them onto the range top, and between the sunshine and the incredible smells and her hair, glorious in the sunshine, Matt thought he'd die. "So I noticed."

He leaned over the egg casserole, inhaling deeply enough to get a whiff of Kelly as well, then straightened, sliding his gaze to the sweatshirt. "This almost makes up for that hideous thing."

On an affronted gasp, she looked down at the shirt, pulling the fabric tightly enough across her front that he almost imagined her saw her nipples outlined on either side of "Est. 1856." "Don't listen to him, Gertie," she whispered, "you're beautiful exactly as you are—"

"You name your sweatshirts?"

"Only this one," she said with an unapologetic shrug, then lugged the first casserole over to the small table next to the window. "She's gotten me through some tough times, Gertie has."

"And is this one of those times?" Matt said quietly, and Kelly turned, her hands knotted in front of her.

"Breakfast first," she said, and hope took a header.

But in the good-news department...at least there was bacon, right?

Kelly wrapped her hands around her warm mug—had to give the man props, he did have decent coffee—and smiled as she watched him finish off his third helping of the egg casserole. Not that she'd exactly picked at her food, either—she hadn't been kidding about being starving. She'd also hoped against hope that eating would fuel her brain as it filled her stomach. At least enough to sort out a thing or six rattling around in there.

So much for Lynn's fling theory.

Of course, all along there'd been options, not to initiate last night's funfest to begin with topping the list. But even after Kelly had set that little scenario in motion, she could have changed her mind. Or slunk away in the wee hours like a coward. Or, this morning, pretended that everything was completely fine, which seemed more stupid than courageous. So this was her compromise—sticking around, making breakfast. Addressing issues.

And this quietly amazing man had been gracious enough to simply sit down and eat his breakfast, biding his time, not pressing her for answers he must have guessed she didn't yet have, or at least wasn't ready to talk about. Instead they'd chatted about ordinary stuff, such as his imminent return to work, and her menu for that night's event—even the weather, for heaven's sake—as though today was no different than yesterday.

As though she was.

In the surprisingly comfortable, if pregnant, silence that had settled between them, Kelly lowered her mug to the table, fingers still clamped around the handle as she rested her chin in her hand and watched him. She wasn't going to lie and say there'd never been afterglows with Rick, because of course there had, at least at the beginning. Heck, she'd been so new at all of it *any* sex was good sex at that point. Took her some years to realize there was more to that side of things than she was getting. That she wanted more, and not only in bed.

And there was Mr. More himself, sitting right in front of her. Someone who redefined the concepts of attentive and unselfish and giving. Someone she trusted completely. Someone she knew she could count on, who'd probably do anything for her—within legal limits, anyway.

So why the niggles? Why, as amazing as last night had been, did something feel off…?

"You're doing it again," Matt said quietly, wiping his mouth and leaning back, arms crossed high on his chest, and she knew her reprieve was over.

"Doing what?"

"Thinking."

"Oh, and you don't think?"

"Not as loudly as you do." Then he smiled, held out his hand and said, "Time to talk," when she put her hand in his. And, yep, she could feel it again, even stronger, that old pull she'd fought and fought and fought since her return to Maple River, to let Matt be whatever he wanted to be, to be her *everything,* because she was tired, dammit, of carrying the load all by herself. Tired of making all the decisions, tired of holding her breath for fear she'd make the wrong call, screw up her kids…tired of not having anyone else to talk to. Other than Lynn, that was, who'd lost her son, for God's sake, and didn't need a whiny, insecure daughter-in-law to deal with on top of her own grief.

"I'm a little freaked out right now," she said, because it was the truth and he deserved no less. But now the tears searing her eyes were angry ones.

His gaze locked in hers, Matt gently squeezed her hand. "Because of…?"

"Everything." Matt lifted one brow. "You have no idea, how many times last night I…lost myself in you. In what we were doing."

"Actually, I do. But this is a problem why?"

"I'm serious, Matt—"

"I know you are. Except— Oh, hell, get over here."

She hesitated, then got up to sit on his lap, where he looped his arms around her waist. "Call me crazy, but I think that's how it's supposed to work. That losing-yourself thing." He smiled, but it was slightly off-kilter, not his usual cocky smile.

"So…you've felt like that before?"

Something flickered in his eyes. Maybe. "Before you? No."

"Oh, come on—"

"What? You think I'm blowing up your skirt?" His gaze darkened. "I don't do that, Kelly. Which I would've thought you'd've figured out by now. So yeah—last night shook me up, too. And don't give me that face, like you don't believe me, because it's true. And you're right. It is scary. Scary as hell. And you know why?"

Wasn't as if she didn't know the answer to this one. "Because it's about giving up control."

"Exactly," he said, giving her waist a squeeze. "And you and me… We both have good reason not to want to do that. So when I woke up this morning and thought you'd left…it wasn't a good feeling, believe me. Because for a moment, I thought I'd failed you."

Her mouth fell open. "Did you not hear me last night? How on earth could you have possibly thought you'd failed?"

"I didn't say *I* failed," he said, with a lopsided grin, "I said failed *you.* And that has nothing to do with making you scream your brains out…." He sighed. "Sorry, that sounded really crass—"

"Why?" she said on a short laugh. "Since you did. And I did." She paused. "Speaking of firsts."

"That is so sad," he said, and a soft laugh popped from her mouth.

"You're telling me. But I don't get—"

"Okay, let me try this again. When you showed up last night, hell, even before, when you called—" he gave his head a shake "—I knew how hard it was for you to take that step. And I felt—" his hand landed on his chest "—humbled. Like you'd given me this precious chance to, I don't know. Do whatever you needed me to do, be whoever you needed me to be. Like…"

He touched her cheek, his gaze so earnest it almost hurt to look at. "Like nothing less than my A game was gonna cut it. That I really had to *think* about what was happening, what I wanted to happen, instead of simply going with the flow."

"Oh, Matt..." Horrified, Kelly cupped his rough cheeks. "I never meant to make you feel that pressured—"

"Not pressured. More like...highly motivated."

Even as she laughed, her eyes stung again. Then, on another exhale, she rested her cheek in his hair. "You can't help being who you are, being protective. But...that's also what makes you so dangerous for me," she said softly, and she felt him tense. She lifted her head to look into Matt's face, smiling as she smoothed her fingertips over his creased forehead. "Because I still honestly don't know if I'm strong enough to withstand your...pull."

"And I told you, I'd never push you into something you weren't ready for—"

"Then I suppose I should give you a chance to prove that, huh?"

Confusion played over his features for a moment or two before a smile bloomed. "You sure?"

In answer, even though she wasn't sure at all, even though her stomach was quaking, Kelly grabbed the hem of her sweatshirt and whisked it over her head, her hair crackling madly around her face and shoulders when she tugged it off. Matt's nostrils flared, his mouth going slack, and at that moment she felt...empowered. In charge.

And let's go with that, shall we?

"I don't do this for just anybody, you know," she said, and he laughed and gently pushed her up and off his lap, letting the dog outside on their way back to the bedroom. Except she yanked him to a halt in the living room, ablaze in the morning sun.

Matt turned, frowning. Slightly. Then one eyebrow lifted. "Here? Really?"

Grinning through the nerves, Kelly dug a condom out of her jeans' pocket and tossed it to Matt, who caught it one-handed. Then, in the spotlight of brilliant sunshine, she toed off her sneakers and wriggled out of her pants. Kicked them to the side. Took a moment to savor the delicious cocktail of chilled air and hot sun and her lover's gaze prickling her skin before closing the few feet between them and lacing her fingers behind his neck.

"Really," she said, and Matt's hands were in her hair, and he was kissing her as though he'd just been let out of prison, leaving her dizzy. Then, somehow, he was on his knees, slowly scraping his whiskers across the tender skin of her belly, and she made a sound that was half gasp, half growl, which made him laugh in turn before carefully lowering to her to the soft, sun-heated area rug, like a glowing red jewel in the midst of the gleaming, golden floor.

And in that instant, everything shifted. Like freaking *sand.*

Never mind that, again, it had been her call. That, again, she'd opened to *him.* Except this time, when Matt's gaze hooked Kelly's as she took him inside, her surrender—to him, to the moment, to fate, what*ever*—was so complete and soul shattering, her hunger for him so rapacious that all she could think in that split second before she sailed over the edge was *Oh, hell.*

Because *want* and *need* had just gotten so tangled up in her brain, she had no idea what either of them meant anymore.

Chapter Ten

By mid-April, Matt—and apparently everybody else at Home Depot that Sunday afternoon—was finally beginning to believe spring might actually stick around for more than ten minutes.

"But you probably shouldn't plant petunias yet," Kelly said beside him as he pushed his—their?—cart through the garden center that smelled of roses and fertilizer and damp soil. He'd mentioned fixing up the yard and she'd taken the bait. Thank God, since he knew diddly about plants. "It's too early, we could still have another storm that'd freeze them."

True enough. Craziest winter ever, with more snow this year than in the previous four or five combined. Last blizzard had only been the week before, in fact, decimating the cherry tree blossoms that, because of the insane warm spell the week before that, had decided to bloom early.

"Hey, guys," she called out to the kids, who were fascinated by the display of fountains at the end of the aisle. A breeze danced in her hair, twisted her long, colorful skirt around her legs. "Don't go any farther, okay?"

Matt smiled at Coop's dismissive yeah-yeah wave, at Kelly's mother-henning, despite feeling that, like the weather, he didn't dare trust what was happening here, either. He wasn't totally clueless—he'd picked up that something was off after they'd made love on his living room floor that morning. That things still didn't feel quite right.

Even though it wasn't like they didn't get along fine, because they did. All of them, the kids included. In fact, when the munchkins had been with their grandmother again last weekend, it'd been Kelly's suggestion they spend it together, snuggling up to him in her bed on Sunday morning, naked and warm and raring to go. Except that was when it hit him that she was trying too damn hard to *make* this work. Unfortunately so was he, twisting himself inside out to be whomever, whatever, she needed him to be…even if he still wasn't sure what that was—

"Pansies," she said, hiking her purse up on her shoulder and tromping over to a display of yellow and purple and white flowers, then holding out what she'd called a six-pack. And her smile sent shivers up his spine, like it always did. "That's what you need."

No, what Matt needed was to feel like he knew what the hell was going on here.

Not that he wasn't grateful for her efforts—oh, so grateful—but somewhere along the way that whole *honesty* thing had gone out the window, which was beginning to irk him to no end. Especially since that was what'd tanked his marriage, that he and Marcia had never been entirely upfront with each other. Or happy, really.

Leaning heavily on the cart's handle, Matt watched Kelly scoot up and down the aisles, frowning slightly as she poked through the plants, apparently searching for the most flawless specimens available. Like perfection was even possible.

Only as a grinning Kelly swished back to the cart, both hands laden with bobbing baby flowers, Matt reminded himself that she *had* been upfront with him all along about the risks. That she was still working stuff out in her head, that he'd have to be patient with her.

Then she zipped away again, this time to the kids, where she squatted to gather her daughter to her side, completely oblivious to Aislin's tangling her fat little fingers in Kelly's curls as she and Coop discussed the merits of the various fountains. And his heart swelled at all that love in her eyes, her voice, for her children, as that Bible verse his mother liked to quote popped into his head. Something about… patience having her perfect work?

And Matt hauled in a deep, deep breath and thought, *Here's hoping.*

Later, in the midst of gouging holes for all those pansies alongside the front walk, Matt glanced up to see his father, in his standard TV-dad cardigan and ball cap, moseying toward the house. Like dropping in unannounced was something he did on a regular basis.

His brow knotted, Matt rocked back on his heels, dragging his henley sleeve across his damp forehead. "Pop! What…?"

"It's a nice day," he said with a shrug. "Figured I'd better get in a walk before Mother Nature gets all pissy again." The Colonel nodded toward Matt's attempt at landscaping, slipping his hands in his pockets. "Looks good. Reminds me of our yard. When your mother…" He paused, frowning slightly, then repeated, "It looks good."

"Thanks," Matt muttered, getting to his feet, only then

noticing a weary slump to his father's shoulders he'd never seen before. Hell. "Come on up, have a seat—"

"Nah, you're busy—"

"I'm digging holes. I think I can talk and do that at the same time."

After a moment, his dad nodded, then started up the walk. "If you're sure it's no bother," he said, and suddenly Matt saw through the tiny chink in the man's nearly impervious armor that he still hadn't recovered from losing his wife, only he was too damn stubborn to admit it.

"Sit, Pop," he said gently. "You want a soda or something?"

"Water's fine, thanks. These new?" he said, lowering himself to one of the white Kennedy rockers that had somehow ended up in the back of the SUV with the flowers.

"Yep. Today, in fact. Kelly helped picked them out." Actually, Matt remembered as he ducked inside to grab a water bottle from the fridge, she'd pointed and said, "You need these," and he hadn't argued.

"How's that working out?" his father said when Matt returned and handed over the condensation-beaded bottle. Kelly and the kids had visited the Colonel a couple times after he'd gotten back, so he knew all the pertinent details behind her return to Maple River. That she was renting the basement apartment. But that was all. And Matt intended to keep it that way until… Well, until there was something to say, he supposed.

"Good," he said, bouncing down the steps to continue his chore. "Alf's in heaven, having kids to play with." Lying in the shade of the front yard's lone tree, a twenty-five-foot maple heavy with seeds, the dog lifted her head, groaned and laid back down again.

"I take it Kelly's not here?"

"No, she and the chicks went to Target. I said I'd rather

chew off my right arm than go anywhere near there on a Sunday."

His father chuckled. "Don't blame you. She help pick out the flowers, too?"

"Yeah, actually." He popped another young, bright yellow plant out of its black-plastic bed, tucked it into the warm soil, where the little pansy faces seemed to grin up at him. Or stick out their tongues. "Since what I know about gardening you could write on a matchbook."

"So...you think she's going to stick around?"

"Have no idea," Matt said over the twist in his gut. "Although I doubt a basement apartment is part of her long-term plan."

"And I'd say you're probably right," his father said in a funny voice. His brows pulled together, Matt looked over his shoulder at him.

"What's that supposed to mean?"

The water bottle set on a small iron table beside the rocker, his father abandoned the rocker to sit on the porch's top step, removing his hat to dangle it between his knees. "I guess I can understand why Kelly moved back to Maple River. But since this town is lousy with apartments, she didn't have to live in your basement, did she? Now she's picking out porch furniture. And plants. And clearly you were expected to go along on the Target junket, but you declined." His shoulders hitched. "You can't be that blind, boy. And if you are, I'm sure as hell not."

Matt laughed out loud. "You think she's—"

"Got an eye on moving upstairs," his father said, blue eyes twinkling. "So you might want to keep an eye on *that.*"

As Matt gawked at him, his brain having apparently gone offline, his father palmed his salt-and-pepper hair, then said, very softly, "I know what's it like, son. The..."

He frowned at the hat, then lifted his eyes back to Matt. "The damned *emptiness*. And that emptiness... Sometimes it plays with your head. Makes you vulnerable. And you find yourself thinking, wouldn't it be nice to fill all that empty space...?"

"That's not what's going on here," Matt said, because obviously his mouth had come back online before his brain, and he thought, *Damn it.* Especially when it occurred to him, a second and a lifetime later, that he didn't actually know whose emptiness his father meant—Matt's or Kelly's.

"Then what is?" his father asked, and Matt balked. Like always. Hell, he was still even selective about what he shared with Kelly, although that was partly because he figured she had enough going on in her own head, she didn't need to deal with his crap, too. But he could tell from the way Pop was looking at him that circumventing the topic wasn't going to work, in no small part because he knew how much Kelly meant to the old man.

Who obviously hadn't ambled over here to talk about gardening.

Another moment passed, however, before Matt joined his father. And, after a few stops and starts, told him everything. Well, almost everything. Not about the sex, obviously, but about Kelly's fears and Matt's wondering if he was, in fact, a fool for hoping...or if that message he'd gotten about patience was worth heeding. And Pop listened, poker-faced, mulling all of it over for some time before saying, "So you love her."

After a moment, Matt breathed out, "Yeah."

"You tell her that?"

"And scare her off? Hell, no."

"Huh." His father tapped his hat against the edge of the step. "But you're friends, yes?"

"I'd like to think so."

"And her kids… You like them?"

He thought of Coop, such a goofy amalgamation of silly and serious, of Aislin's unfettered joy, and smiled. "You have no idea."

"And they're okay with you?"

"Seems that way."

"And you're sure that's not just the emptiness talking? I mean, after what that…*woman* put you through—"

Matt's brows dipped. He'd never told his father the details behind his breakup. "How do you know about—"

"As I said, I'm not blind. So?"

"I don't know," Matt said on a rush of air. "Maybe it is. But…is it so wrong to want to fill the void? If the time's right?"

"I'd say that depends on the woman."

"Hey. It was you who brought up her helping me buy plants and porch furniture, remember?"

"So I might've been off-base there," the Colonel said, and Matt released a dry laugh. Then he sighed.

"So…what are you saying, Pop? Now, I mean?" His eyes cut to his father's. "That I should give up?"

After a moment, the Colonel palmed the space between Matt's shoulder blades, shocking him. Physically demonstrative, the old man wasn't. And damned if there wasn't a softness in his eyes he'd never seen before, either. "Don't get me wrong—I like Kelly. A lot. And I appreciate what she's been through. But you're my son. Meaning I'm not real keen on seeing you go through hell again. Like you said, these things can't be forced. I'm not saying it doesn't take a lot of work to keep the spark lit, but if it feels too hard to light it to begin with…"

He gave Matt's back a pat, then looked back out over the yard. "If you're not absolutely sure this is going to pan out, you might want to consider cutting your losses. Before things get any messier. Especially for the kids."

Then Kelly's van turned into their street, and despite everything his father had said, Matt's heart rate sped up at the thought of seeing her again. Of sharing the mundane things, like eating dinner and reading to Aislin, of walks to the park as the kids rode their bikes, of trolling the aisles at Home Depot....

So what if it wasn't perfect? What relationship was?

Or maybe Pop was right, if it was this hard to keep the spark lit—

Van in driveway, everyone out of the car, Kelly came over, smiling, arms outstretched. Not to hug Matt, but the Colonel, who'd gotten to his feet. A huge hug, like only Kelly could give.

"Stay for dinner?" she said to his father, her eyes crinkled as she kept hold of his arms. When he demurred, she shook her head. Laughing. "Pork chops. Already defrosted, easy-peasy. You can't say no."

And as Matt stood there, watching, he knew, without a doubt, why he loved her. With everything he had in him.

Meaning he also knew, without a doubt, that half-assed wasn't gonna cut it.

Not anymore.

"So you gonna tell me what's going on between you and my brother or do I have to come out to Jersey and smack it out of you?"

Sabrina's exasperation vibrating in her ear, Kelly wandered out onto the porch, her forehead scrunched so hard it hurt. It was a perfect spring evening, slightly breezy, not too cool. As anyone with half a brain would think her life was right now. Perfect, that is. Or as close to perfect as it got. Her kids were healthy and happy, business was good and Matt…

Oh, dear God. Matt.

Sighing, Kelly sank onto the top step, tugging her long tiered skirt around her legs. Matt, kids and dog had walked the Colonel back to his house, although they'd return at any moment. Nearby a robin sang its heart out. Probably to its mate.

Not helping, she thought, her eyes watering.

"He wasn't supposed to say anything. Not until…we were sure."

Bree snorted. "Yeah, well, he did. Although to give him credit I don't think he meant to spill the beans, they just kinda fell out of his mouth."

"And what 'beans,' exactly, did he spill?"

"That the two of you have been together for a few weeks. Except he didn't sound nearly as happy about that as I would've expected. And neither do you, chickie."

"And what am I supposed to say? You're not exactly an impartial third party. Matt's your twin, for heaven's sake—"

"And for a long, long time," Bree gently said, "you were my sister. By choice. Do I think this is a little weird? Hell, yeah. But I love you both. And if either of you is hurting, so am I."

"Which is why we'd agreed to keep this between us for the time being." Kelly blew out a breath. "There's nothing you can do—"

"Except listen. Which I actually do now. As opposed to when we were kids and… God. How on earth did you stand it, listening to me yammer on about myself for hours on end?"

"What can I say?" Kelly said, smiling. "You were very…entertaining."

Another snort, then Sabrina said, "Well, now I owe you. So start talking." At Kelly's silence, she added gently, "You know you can trust me. Because I can keep my mouth shut." She chuckled. "These days, anyway."

So Kelly sucked in a lungful of air and dived in, admitting that no matter how hard she tried to shove the fear away, it wouldn't go. That, in fact, the harder she fell for Matt, the closer fear pressed that it was still too soon, the danger of losing herself again too real, that the man was too damn protective—Bree grunted, agreeing—and if Kelly couldn't appreciate that, appreciate *him,* how on earth was this ever going to work?

"Good point," Bree said, but now that Kelly had let loose the hounds, there was no calling them back.

"And worse is that I can tell Matt's so afraid of saying or doing the 'wrong' thing that we're *both* holding back, and how unfair is that? Not to mention, well, dishonest. To all of us. Especially the kids, who…" Her eyes filled. "Who're growing more attached every day."

"As are you," her friend said softly, and Kelly gave a shaky sigh.

"I don't get it, Bree. How can something feel so damn close to right, and yet…" She exhaled loudly. "So…I found this little rental house the other day," she said.

"Oh, honey… Really?" Bree responded.

"Yeah." It was a sweet little house, really. Still close to Coop's school, and her professional kitchen. Nice yard. They could get a dog, if Coop wanted—

At the end of the block, the gang appeared, Linnie doing her little wiggle skip as she held Matt's hand, Coop gesturing wildly as he told Matt some story or other, and she felt as though she'd been knifed.

"I think it's best," she said to Bree. "And they're right up the block, I've got to go."

"We'll talk," her friend said, and disconnected.

Coop ran toward Kelly, yelling, "Mom! Matt said if it's okay with you, I can ride my bike for a little bit!"

Kelly squinted at the coral sun rapidly sinking toward the horizon. "A little bit is right. It's almost dark—"

"I know, I know—"

"And wear your gear!"

"Sheesh, Mom," he said, huffing a huge sigh as he and Matt headed toward the garage and Linnie bounced up the porch steps, crawled into her lap and promptly plugged her thumb into her mouth.

"Sleepy girl?" Kelly murmured, stroking her baby's soft curls. At her little girl's nod, Kelly shoved to her feet—*my gosh, this kid is getting heavy!*—and carried her insidc to get ready for bed, blinking back tears as she wondered how she was going to tell Matt they were leaving. Without breaking his heart, that is.

You'd think, after Rick, she'd be better at ending things.

But no.

"I *hate* wearing all this stuff," Cooper said as Matt fixed the strap on Coop's bike helmet. How it kept getting loose, Coop had no idea. "I feel like a robot!"

Squatting in front of him, Matt smiled, then handed him back the helmet. With a sigh, Coop put it on, snapped the strap. At least it was cool looking, a dark, glittery blue. But now that the weather was warmer it itched. And the knee and elbow pads were a pain.

"Better to feel like a robot than hurting your noggin," Matt said with a light tap on the helmet's top, which made Coop grin. He couldn't even remember why he'd been so worried about Matt, because now he liked him. A lot. Like how he always talked in a quiet voice. The way his eyes crinkled when he smiled. And how he never acted like

Coop was bothering him when he asked him something. "Or scraping your knees and elbows if you fall."

"Except I never do! Ever! You've seen me, I'm a good rider!"

"And even the best riders wear their protective gear. And you've got maybe fifteen minutes before the sun's down," he said, standing, and Coop sighed again.

"Will you watch me?"

"Like a hawk," Matt said, and Coop pushed off down the sidewalk, looking out for where tree roots had shoved up the cement. He'd love to ride in the street, where it was smooth. But Mom said he wasn't big enough to do that yet.

She never let him do anything, sheesh.

He reached the end of the block, looped around to come back. Lots of people were out, walking their dogs and stuff. From what felt like really far away, he saw Matt wave to him. Coop raised one hand to wave back, right as a pair of giggling girls passed. The end of the handlebar stung his hand when he grabbed it, but even though he wobbled a little when he hit a bump, trying to get out of their way, he was okay.

Except then some dog came out of nowhere, rushing him and barking its head off. Startled, Coop jerked the bike so he wouldn't hit the dog, only he bounced over a tree root, then off the iron fence right beside him, and the next thing he knew he was flying....

His heart in his throat, Matt sprinted down the street, Alf at his heels, both reaching Coop as the boy slowly pulled himself into a sitting position. With a "Thanks, I've got this," Matt waved off a concerned neighbor, then shoved the worried dog out of the way to get a closer look at the kid. Who wasn't crying or in obvious pain, although his lower lip was quivering a little. Winded and a little stunned would be his guess. "You okay?"

"I...th-think so. Stupid dog—"

"I saw." Heaving a sigh, Matt glanced down the street at the rapidly vanishing mutt. He doubted the thing was dangerous, simply out for a little adventure, but still. He turned back to Coop. "Believe me, that owner's gonna get a visit from me.... Hey, buddy," he said gently, cupping the little boy's shoulder when the lip quivering got worse. "What is it...?"

"I d-didn't mean to... The b-bike..." Coop looked over at the crippled bike, scrubbing a tear off his dirty cheek. "I'm sorry, I should've been more careful. Dad—"

A memory flashed from when Matt was five, when he accidentally knocked his father's boom box onto the unforgiving tile floor, shattering it—

What the hell's wrong with you? Are you blind? Or just stupid...?

Silently swearing, Matt yanked Coop against his chest, the boy's quiet tears ripping him to shreds. "It's okay, buddy.... It was an accident." Then he gently pulled Coop away, capturing the teary gaze in his. "Not your fault, okay? Bikes can be fixed." He glanced over, sighed then looked back at Coop, smiling. "Or replaced. What matters is that *you're* all right—"

"Oh, my God, Coop!" Panting, Kelly dropped to her knees on the pavement, reeking of fear. "Are you all right, sweetie?"

"Yeah, mostly." He straightened his glasses, gave Matt a small smile then crinkled his nose at his mom. "Did you leave Linnie alone?"

"Of course not. She's asleep, Mrs. Otero is with her. For heaven's sake, what are you doing?" she said when Coop tried to stand. "Stay still, something could be broken—"

"He's fine, Kelly—"

"You don't know that!" Kelly responded. "So how's about letting me take care of my own kid, okay?" Then, wide-eyed, she clamped a hand over her mouth. As Coop's eyes darted back and forth between them, she shook her head, tears cresting before she lowered her hand again. "I'm so sorry, I didn't mean—"

"No problem," Matt said, very quietly, as he got to his feet. And part of him—the pissed-as-hell part—was briefly tempted to walk away, to let the stubborn woman handle it all on her own, just like she wanted. Except even Ms. Pigheaded had to admit there was no way she could get a banged-up kid and his even worse banged-up bike home on her own.

He looked at Coop, who was testing his legs. Limping a little, but probably otherwise okay. "*Can* you walk?" Matt asked.

"Yeah. It hurts, sorta. But not bad, I swear," he said, when Kelly mashed her lips together.

"I could carry you," Matt said, and horror streaked across the kid's face.

"No!" Then he looked at the bike, trying so hard not to start crying again. "But…"

Matt grabbed the bike by its frame, hefting it up to his side. "Like I said, if it can't be fixed I'll get you another one."

"You don't have to—" Kelly began, but Matt quelled her with what was probably not the kindest look in the world. Because he knew what she was thinking, that who bought the next bike was immaterial, because there wasn't going to be a next bike. Because God forbid she let the kid take a few risks.

Because God forbid, he thought, seeing the regret in her eyes, *she* take any.

But that was her decision. Just like it'd been all along. Terms he'd agreed to; no point in moaning about them now.

"Discussion closed," he said, going ahead, letting her guide her hobbling son back to the house.

House. Not *home.*

Kelly knew Matt was waiting for her. Waiting for the talk they'd both put off for too long. Fortunately Mrs. Otero was happy to stick around, especially when Kelly sweetened the deal—literally—with a promise of assorted bite-size desserts left over from yesterday's event, which her clients hadn't wanted.

He was on the porch, his hands folded across his stomach, sitting in the rocker but not rocking. Alf lifted her head at Kelly's approach, her tail thumping against the floorboards. Kelly came only as far as the top step, though, where she sat so she wouldn't have to look at him. Not that she could see him all that well, anyway, in the dark, the nighttime breeze braiding with the sweet scents of grape-scented hyacinths and newly mown grass, the tang of charred meat from somebody's barbeque—

"This isn't working, honey," he said behind her, very softly. "For either of us."

Now she turned, trying to see his face. Needing to. "I'm so sorry, Matt. You know how much I wanted it to."

"Really?" he said, and for the first time she heard the anger that must've been simmering for weeks. And her own flared.

"I did warn you, Matt. That I wasn't sure if I could do this—"

"Dammit, Kelly—" he sighed "—I have bent over backward to prove I'm not trying to control you, or clip your wings, or whatever it is you're so damned afraid of. That I'm *not Rick*—"

"I know that," she said, her face flaming.

"Then why won't you let me all the way in, no matter what I say? Or do. Why can't you trust me? Fine, so I'd protect you, all of you, with my life, because that's how I was raised. Who I am. That's what a man is *supposed* to do." He hesitated, then said, "Especially when he loves somebody. Loves the woman underneath all the crap, anyway."

She twisted around, frowning. "What did you say?"

"Yeah. Deal. And I never said it before because... because God forbid I *pressure* you. But now it's like what the hell, since treading lightly didn't work, anyway. I don't get it, Kell. I honest to God don't. Why you see me protecting you guys as such a threat. Especially since you're exactly the same way. With the kids, I mean."

He had a point. "I don't get it, either," she said quietly, as she turned back around, her chest feeling as though Alf was standing on it. "Because I love you, too. Have for some time, actually. And I do trust you. I know you'd never hurt us."

The boards squeaked when Matt leaned forward. "Then, sweetheart," he asked, so gently she cringed, "what the *hell* is the problem?"

Kelly leaned her head against the post next to the stairs. The robin bid the world good-night, a sweet sound that made her want to cry. "You know what I don't trust? Life. Because every time I'd thought things were going pretty good before, I got slapped in the face." She paused. "Literally, at one point."

Silence reverberated behind her. "You said he never physically abused you."

"Actually, I sidestepped the question, as I recall. Because it was only once, and years ago. And he never lifted a hand to me again. I swear. And, yes," she said softly, "Linnie was the result of her father's...apology."

"Damn it, Kelly—why didn't you tell me all of this that first night? Especially since I gave you the opening—"

"I don't know! Okay? I was flying on adrenaline, and instinct, and…maybe the doubts were already creeping in about that phone call, that I'd heard wrong, misconstrued Rick's words. Or maybe because it *had* been four years, and if the court didn't take it that seriously, why even bring it up? Or…" She shook her head and said softly, "Or maybe, just maybe, because I was too ashamed to admit I'd stayed with a man who'd hit me."

"You thought I'd *judge* you?"

"People do," she said wearily. "Besides, *who* went to his sister the next morning to see if my story held up? It's okay," she said, interrupting whatever he'd been about to say. "You're a cop, we hadn't seen each other in years, you had no idea if I was telling the truth or not. You did what you had to do—"

"To protect *you* as much as—"

"Yourself? I know. No, really, I do. Except then it was all moot, wasn't it? But the thing is…stuff happens. One minute it's all rainbows and kittens and then boom. Somebody dies, or turns out not to be who you thought they were, and…" Her shoulders bumped.

"And you survive," Matt said, his voice sharp. "You learn from it and buck up and move on."

Kelly whipped around. "But how can I do that as long as you're doing the bucking up for me? And if I'm afraid to let you do that, to be *you,* if I—we—can't find that balance… we have an unsolvable problem." She pressed a hand to her chest. "I'm so, so sorry, but it just seems to me we shouldn't have to think so hard, try so hard, to *make* this work. God knows we've got the surface stuff down, but…if we can't be who we really are, then what's the point?"

When he didn't say anything, she swallowed. "Once before, I fought for something I finally had to admit wasn't meant to be. I'm not saying this is anything even remotely like that situation, because it's not…but I won't do that again. Not to me, not to the kids. Or to you. So it's like you said, sometimes all you can is buck up and move on." She hesitated, then said, "I…I found another place."

A moment, then several more, passed. From down the street, she heard laughter from a newlywed couple on their porch, a dog barking. Alf lifted her head, listening.

"I see," Matt finally said. "Where?"

"Not f-far…" Kelly squeezed her eyes shut, waiting, then said, "It seemed…best." Then she pushed herself to her feet, hugging herself against the nighttime chill. The pain. "It's like you s-said—" her teeth began to chatter "—you n-need, and deserve, someone who can let you all the way in. Who can let *g-go.* Apparently I'm not that person. No matter how much I want to be."

Then, before he could say something, anything, to change her mind, she raced down the steps, barely making it around the side of the house before she sank into the soft, damp earth between the brand-new flowerbeds, covering her mouth to mask her sobs.

Chapter Eleven

Coop waited until Mrs. Otero left before coming out of his room, where he found Mom curled up on the sofa in the dark. Well, almost dark, the light over the stove was on, but that wasn't saying much. She was just sitting there, not watching TV or anything. She kinda jerked when she realized he'd come in, then blew her nose.

"What are you doing up, sweetie? Are you okay…?"

"Mostly, yeah." He sat in the big chair, but only on the edge, so the balls of his feet touched the floor. "Mrs. Otero says kids're made of rubber—they bounce right back when they get hurt."

He thought maybe Mom smiled. "And wouldn't it be wonderful if that were true? Come here," she said, patting the space beside her. "We need to talk."

He sure didn't like the sound of that. But he went, anyway, smushing himself against Mom's side when she put her arm around him. "I found us our own house," she said into his hair. "With a yard and everything. And it's closer to school, so you can even walk if you want—"

"Wait." Coop sat up, looking at Mom's face. "We're *moving? Again?*"

"At the beginning of the month, yes. And as I said, there's a yard, so we could get a dog—"

"I already have a dog. Alf."

"Honey…" Mom touched his hair. "Alf's Matt's dog. So she'd stay here."

Suddenly, his stomach hurt. "Did you and Matt have a fight?"

She laughed, but it sounded totally fake. "Of course not—"

"You're lying!"

"Coop!"

"You had a fight, and then you broke up, like you and Dad did, and now—"

His eyes felt hot and stingy. He tried to back away, but Mom wrapped him up tight in her arms again. *Really* tight. "There's nothing 'just like me and your father' about this," she whispered. "Matt and I… It's not like that."

"You can say that again."

After a moment, she let him go, only to catch his chin in her fingers and make him look at her. "Say what again?"

"That you and Matt aren't anything like you and Dad were. Because him and you… It was better. *Is* better. Like, a million, zillion times better. He makes you *laugh,* Mom." He slumped against the sofa cushions, feeling a little like he might throw up, like everything was getting turned upside down *again.* "He makes *me* laugh. I feel good, when he's around. And…and safe."

"Oh, baby… I know." She swallowed. "Believe me, I know."

Tears bunching in his eyes, Coop looked at her again.

"Then why do we have to leave? Why can't we stay right here and you and Matt could get married so we could be a real family?"

"Married?"

"Yeah, married. I mean, wouldn't that make sense?"

Mom let out a huge sigh that almost sounded like a laugh. "Sweetie…people don't—or at least, shouldn't—get married simply because, in some ways, it makes sense. There's more to it than that."

"Like what?"

She pulled him close and kissed the top of his head. "Like all kind of things eight-year-old boys aren't ready to understand. And definitely shouldn't be worrying about. Look… I'm glad you like Matt so much. Really glad. His whole family… They're great people. *Good* people. And you can see him and the Colonel and Abby anytime you want, I promise."

"Really?"

"Yes, really." She stroked his hair for a moment, then said, "I know a lot more now than I did when I married your father. Or at least I'd like to think I do. And one of those things is that for two people to be together, it has to feel…right. Really right, way deep inside. From the very beginning. And…Matt deserves more than I can be for him right now. You'll just have to trust me on this." She messed with his hair some more, then said, "And you need to get back to bed—you have school tomorrow."

"Like I'm gonna be able to sleep."

"Maybe…some hot chocolate would help?"

Knowing he was making his grumpy face, Coop pushed himself off the sofa. "Hot chocolate's not gonna fix this one, Mom," he said, then tromped back to his room.

From behind the U-Haul backed up to Kelly's "new" house, Matt heard a car door slam. Seconds later a brief, humorless laugh preceded a gravelly voice. "You do realize that most landlords don't help their tenants move? Especially *out?*"

Grunting, Matt dragged Aislin's mattress down the loading plank and across the small yard. Kelly had mentioned her former mother-in-law was coming to keep an eye on Linnie, but Matt hadn't expected to get the third degree the minute the woman arrived.

"Was that supposed to be a reply?" she called behind him.

Matt set the mattress inside the open door, returned to the truck for the box spring.

"Only one I got."

"Pity. Because that one sucks." Her purse hanging from her shoulder, she crossed toned, tan arms over her sleeveless blouse. Tiny, but tough. Like a fox terrier his mother had once had. "I take it Kelly and the kids aren't here?"

"Nope. Kelly and Coop are over at the other house, packing the van while Linnie naps. And you're early."

"Oh, I wouldn't say that," Lynn said, smiling, and Matt thought, *Hell.* Fine, so to most people—as in, sane ones—this probably looked a little bizarre. Okay, very bizarre. But after his and Kelly's little chat ten days ago, it occurred to him it was one thing to release the woman from a commitment or promise or whatever she probably shouldn't have made to begin with, and another thing entirely to abandon her—and the kids—altogether. He could give her space without giving her grief.

Then Lynn picked up a small cooler she'd set down on the short wall bordering the porch steps and said, "I've got beer, want one?" and he thought, *Go, Grandma.*

As well as *Hell,* again.

"I really need to get this set up," he said, heading for the house.

"Five minutes, tops," Lynn said, sitting on the steps, the cooler beside her, and he leaned the box spring up against the side of the house and glowered at the woman. She shrugged and unzipped the cooler.

"Got a problem with German?"

"Nope." Lynn handed Matt a can; he popped the top, then sat beside her. "I suppose you think this is crazy."

"From someone who came to the funeral of a man he'd never met? To support a woman he hadn't seen since they were teenagers?" She laughed. "You tell me. So. What's really going on here?"

Matt took a swallow, then said, "No offense, Lynn… but this is between me and Kelly. Or was. It wouldn't seem right dragging you into it."

"Except, see, I already dragged myself into it." When he frowned at her, she said, "I might've…given Kelly a little push. In your direction. Of course, if she hadn't been already teetering, I could have shoved with the force of Hercules and it wouldn't have done a damn bit of good—"

"*You* were the one behind her…?" He felt his face warm. "How much did she tell you?"

"That she took my suggestion to heart." She tilted her own can to her bare lips, then to him. "And nearly broke hers in the process. Not to mention yours."

"I sincerely doubt her heart is broken. I mean, we're not…together like we were. But I still see her every day. She seems to be doing just fine—"

"'Seems'?"

"Lynn…I appreciate whatever you're trying to do. But talking to me isn't going to change anything. Kell knows I'm here, for her and the kids. Always. But I can't fix whatever's going on inside her head. God knows I would if I could…but I can't. So thanks for the concern, and the beer—" he lifted the can in salute "—but things don't always fall into place the way we'd like—"

"He never fought for her, you know."

Matt frowned. "Who?"

"Rick. Oh, he acted like a petulant child when Kelly left him—the same way he acted when he *was* a child whenever he didn't get his way," she said with a sigh, "but it was always about *him*. How the world had done *him* wrong. He wanted Kelly to be there for him, but he was never there for her. Not in any way that really counted. But Kelly…"

Lynn tilted the can at Matt. "She not only held their marriage together, she held my son together. And when she finally realized she couldn't do that anymore, he fell apart. And unfortunately took part of Kelly with him." A slight frown pushed her brows together. "She's a giver, our Kelly. But from what I gather, I don't think anyone else has ever returned the favor. Or say to her, you matter more to me than anything or anybody else in the world. So no wonder she's on this independence kick. Because the people she should have been able to rely on most all screwed her over. In one way or another."

"I did not screw her over—"

"No. But you sure as hell abandoned her, didn't you?"

Matt flung a hand out toward the moving fan, the mattress leaning against the siding between the windows. "Seriously?"

"Anybody can help somebody move. But you're not exactly putting your ass on the line for her, are you? And she's only trying to cover hers—"

"I told her I love her, for God's sake!"

"And then what did you do? You *graciously* got out of her way."

"Because that's what she wanted! What was I supposed to do? Tell her no?" When Lynn lifted one eyebrow, Matt shook his head. "Sorry, Lynn…but I had my head handed to me on a platter once before because I was 'hovering.' No way am I going down that road again."

Lynn blew out a disgusted *puh.* "Trust me, sweetheart—all that I-need-space malarkey? She doesn't know what she's talking about. It's not space she needs, it's support. So she *can* grow, be what she needs to be. She's never had that, so how the hell does she know what that looks like? And here's a news flash—*telling* somebody you love them doesn't mean a damn thing unless you're willing to make an idiot of yourself. And until you are…"

She shrugged, her words slamming into his head like the butt of a Glock right as Kelly's van pulled into the drive behind the U-Haul. Coop got out first, grinning when he spotted his grandmother before unhooking Linnie from her seat. With a squeal, the little girl scrambled down and over to Lynn as Matt caught Kelly's gaze, seeing in it every bit as much pain and confusion as was probably in his. Because for damn sure whatever they were to each other now, *that* was what wasn't working.

And a blink later, a second revelation skidded into the first—that for all Kelly's protests and rationalizations, she wasn't the problem here.

He was.

A day or so before the move, Kelly had received a "summons," as she thought of it from Coop's teacher that she'd like to speak with Kelly at her earliest convenience. And her initial, guilt-riddled thought had been that the tension between her and Coop since telling him they were leaving Matt's house had translated into problems at school.

But what other choice did she have? she thought as she pulled into the school parking lot. As much as she'd do almost anything for her children, she couldn't pretend everything was fine—that she was—when it wasn't. Been there, done that, had the scars to show for it. And she refused to go there again, not only for her own sake, but also for the kids'. And Matt's.

No matter how much her insides felt scraped out.

Breathing deeply, she crossed the lot, went inside, scribbled her name and the time on the log-in sheet in the school office.

"Room 122, Ms. McNeil," the smiling secretary said. "Mrs. Farmer's expecting you."

"Thanks." Visitor pass in hand, Kelly scurried down the green-and-beige-tiled corridor, the walls plastered with dozens of art projects. She tried to convince her bladder she'd peed not ten minutes ago, she was fine.

Room 122. Glass-paneled door. More artwork displays in the room beyond, very cheerful, really. And there was her son, sitting at a desk in front, working away on something or other. Behind the teacher's desk sat a very pretty dark-skinned woman, her hair a tamed mass of glistening black coils. At Kelly's knock she looked up, breaking into a bright smile. Standing, Mrs. Farmer waved her in and said, "Your mother's here, Cooper," as Kelly entered.

He glanced up, his face expressionless, his glasses crooked. As usual. Kelly resisted the impulse to straighten them. To hug him.

"Have a seat, Ms. McNeil," the teacher said, and Kelly squished herself behind the third-grade-size desk next to her son, folding her hands on top. Leaning back against the front of her own desk, Mrs. Farmer said, "I called you in because there's a discrepancy between Coop's records and the work he's doing in my class."

Guilt sank its claws in even deeper as Kelly glanced over at Coop. But he was focused on his task, seemingly unconcerned. Sighing, Kelly returned her gaze to his teacher.

"I'm…sorry—"

"For what?" Mrs. Farmer said, then softly laughed. "*I'm* sorry for not making myself clear from the get-go. His records indicate he was almost a full year behind at his last school."

"Yes."

"But I gather you homeschooled him for a while?"

"About six months, yes."

"Well, whatever the two of you did during that time? He's so far ahead of his class in his core subjects, I'd like to have him tested for our gifted program."

Kelly's jaw dropped…a moment before panic gripped her so hard she could barely breathe. Frowning slightly, Mrs. Farmer reached behind her and picked up a large envelope from her desk. "Coop? You mind taking this to the office for me?"

"So you and Mom can talk in private?"

"You got it, honey," she said, her laugh a low rumble. With a sharp glance at Kelly, Cooper took the envelope and left, and the teacher smiled again at Kelly. "Coop told me you took him out of school because he was being bullied?"

"I did. It was only verbal, but—"

"Bullying is bullying. Believe me, I know." She crossed her arms, her eyes kind. "You'd hardly be the only mother to do what you did. You do know this school has a zero-tolerance policy against that sort of thing?"

"Oh, trust me, it was one of the first things I asked about."

"I imagine so. And I hope you don't mind, but Coop and I had a long talk about it. About how it's important to realize what those other kids were saying? All lies."

Exactly what she'd tried to tell Cooper. Except with his

father's only reinforcing the…crap, she hadn't been able to make a lot of headway. Not, however, something she felt comfortable sharing with this woman she didn't know, kind eyed or not.

"And now you're worried if he goes into Gifted, he'll get picked on again. I can assure you that won't be an issue."

Kelly blew a sharp breath through her nose. "Can you? Really? Even a zero-tolerance policy—and believe me, I'm grateful for that—doesn't mean it won't happen. Some kids… It's like they look for any excuse to torment someone who's different—"

"But you want the best for your son, right?"

"Of course! And I do understand this could be a wonderful opportunity. I do. But…he's been through so many changes already in the past year or so…." Shaking her head, she glanced toward the bank of windows along the wall, then back at the teacher. "If Coop's doing so well in your class… If he's happy, I mean—"

"He certainly seems to be. And he'd stay right here. If he qualifies, though, there's a supplemental program that would keep him stimulated. Because I'm guessing that child is going to get bored very quickly. And we do not want that, believe me."

"No." Kelly gave a weak smile. "We definitely don't."

Smiling, Mrs. Farmer pushed away from her desk. "You don't have to decide right this second. But why don't we have him tested, take it from there?"

After a moment, Kelly nodded. "Okay. One step at a time, right?"

"Absolutely."

Kelly pried herself from the tiny desk and stood, working the kinks out of her left knee as they walked to the door, where Mrs. Farmer asked, "May I ask you a question?"

"Uh…sure."

"Since things were clearly going so well with the home-schooling, why did you put him back in the classroom setting? I know you're a single mom—it must have been tricky, juggling work and teaching, but if you did it for six months…?"

"It was Coop's idea, actually. Well, after we moved to Maple River."

"Did that surprise you?"

"A little, yes. Especially considering what had happened before. But despite everything, I think he missed…being part of something."

"Gutsy kid," the teacher said, then briefly touched Kelly's arm. "And an even gutsier mama…. Oh, thank you, Coop," she said when the boy returned. "Go on and get your backpack, your mom and I all done here."

"I really like Mrs. Farmer," Kelly said as they walked, their voices echoing in the silent, empty hall. Coop shrugged.

"She's okay. Where's Linnie?"

"Asleep, Mrs. Otero came over. So…that's really neat, huh? About maybe going into the gifted program?"

"I guess."

The handlebar on the big front door *clonked* when Kelly pushed it open. "You don't sound very excited. No, we're not walking, I brought the car," she said when he headed toward the walking path instead of the parking lot.

On a heavy sigh, Coop sharply turned and tromped toward the van, his backpack bouncing on his back. They were in the car, seat belts latched, before Kelly heard behind her, "I don't know if I want to do Gifted."

"Oh? Why?"

"Dunno. I just don't."

"Are you worried? Or scared?"

"Maybe. Yeah."

"Do you know why?"

"Because...what if it's too hard? That's where all the really smart kids are, right?"

"Um...maybe that's why Mrs. Farmer thinks you should give it a shot? Because you *are* one of the smart kids?"

"I don't feel very smart. Not that smart, anyway."

She pulled into their driveway. The house was nice enough, she supposed, if a little bland. Reminding herself it was only a month-to-month rental and someday she'd have her own house again, Kelly got out, waiting for Coop. He came up to her, hanging on to his backpack straps like suspenders, and she looped an arm around his shoulders.

"I think everyone feels they're not as smart, or brave, or strong as they really are...."

She stopped, frowning. "And that's a trap, isn't it?" she said quietly.

As she mentally slapped herself upside the head.

"Huh?" Coop said beside her. Kelly looked down at him, feeling as though fireworks were going off in her brain.

"Come here," she said, leading him to the porch steps. The *wrong* porch steps, she thought, as they sat on the pockmarked cement. "You know how sometimes it feels like there's voices inside our heads, telling us stuff we know better than to listen to? Like...knowing it's bad to eat too much candy, but that little voice tells you to do it, anyway?"

He sheepishly smiled. "Like I did at Easter?"

"Like you did at Easter, exactly. Well, this is kind of like that. Because you do know you're smart. You told me yourself how easy the work was in school now. How you were reading harder books than most of your class. And look how quickly you figured out that LEGO set Matt gave you. All by yourself! Right?" When he nodded, she said, "And you sure as heck are brave, asking to go back to school. And a new school, no less, where you didn't even know anybody."

"Yeah. I guess."

Smiling, Kelly said softly, "But now here's this opportunity to grow, to learn even more, and you're scared to… to take the risk. That you won't be up to the challenge. Only that's not *your* voice telling you that, baby." She swallowed back tears. "It's the fake voice, the one that lies. The one we have to tell to shut up, to get the heck out of our head. The voice that would keep us imprisoned in what we think is…safe."

Coop looked at her for a long, long time, then said, "Like you're scared about being with Matt?"

Kelly snorted. "And you think you're not smart? Please."

He smiled a little at that, then leaned against her arm, which he hadn't done in weeks. "Can I tell you something?"

"Anything," she said, despite thinking, *Oh, God—now what?* "You know that."

After scratching his nose, Coop took a biiig breath and said, very softly, "When Dad died…I wasn't really sad about it."

Her breath caught. "Oh, Coop—"

"I mean, I didn't *want* him dead or anything like that, but…" His chin shook. "I know what you said, about him changing. That he wasn't himself. But whoever he was…" He smashed his lips together, then said in a very small voice, "I didn't like him very much anymore. Because he made me feel bad all the time. What you said? About the voice? That was Dad's voice, telling me I wasn't good enough, or smart enough. Or that I was fat. So after he was gone, I felt like…"

Her eyes stinging, Kelly hugged him closer and whispered, "Like you could breathe again?"

"Yeah," he sighed out.

A tear slipped out as she laid her cheek in his curls. "Sweetie...why on earth didn't you say something?"

Silence shuddered between them before he said, "Because...because I thought everybody would think that was messed up. That *I* was messed up."

Kelly shifted to take Coop's face in her hands, trying to get a lock on his eyes through grimy lenses. "Nobody would *ever* think that. You hear me? There wasn't, and isn't, anything wrong with *you.* Ask your grandmother if you don't believe me."

"Really?"

"Swear to God. And anyone else who might be listening in."

A moment passed before she got a little smile. And a relieved breath. "Okay."

"Okay is right," Kelly said, pulling him to her side again. "And by the way? That took courage to tell me that. So yay you."

She felt him nod against her, then sigh again. "Being scared sucks."

"Won't argue with you there, pookie-bear," she said, and he groaned, making her laugh.

But honestly—how often had she reassured her babies, was still reassuring them, that there were no monsters under the bed or in their closets, that the boogeyman wasn't real? That no matter how nasty or frightening the storm, the sun always came out again? But, yeah, she'd had the voices, too. Rick's, mostly, reinforcing her mother's fears, her father's thinly veiled misogyny.

So some example she was setting. Because the only way to conquer fear was to stand up to it. Plunk a stone in that slingshot and let 'er rip. Instead of, you know, letting the big baddie call the shots.

Let those old voices stand between her and happiness.

You are so going down, she said to her imaginary giant as she dug her cell phone out of her purse, scrolled through her contacts.

"Matt!" Coop yelled, and Kelly thought, *What?* as Matt jerked his car into her driveway. Then he was out, the door slamming shut behind him, his gaze cemented to hers as he strode toward her, a man with a mission, hoo-boy…and a second later she was in his arms, being kissed hard enough to make her dizzy—not to mention deliriously happy, oh, yeah—and she thought, over Coop's war whoop behind them, *Well, okay, then.*

Vaguely, she was aware of Mrs. Otero bursting onto the porch, of Coop's shriek of protest at being herded inside before Matt gathered her close, and it felt so real and right and good she gasped, and that was even before he said, "If you think I'm gonna let you go just because you're scared, you're crazy."

And on a blissful sigh, Kelly squeezed shut her eyes and thought, *This.*

At Kelly's sigh—not to mention how she'd melted into him—Matt released a pent-up breath of his own. Because things could have played out in any number of ways, several of which would have resulted in his ego ending up in the crapper.

But this…this was looking promising. Especially when he took Kelly's hand and tugged her over to the porch steps, and she plopped down beside him, laughing, before snuggling up against him and saying, very softly, "I was about to call you," and a happy little explosion went off in his chest.

"Oh?"

"Yeah. I have been such a goober—"

"Me, too," Matt said, and Kelly sat up, a little crease setting up camp between her brows as she tucked a strand of hair behind her ears.

"How do you figure that?"

Whether he'd ever tell her about his conversation with Lynn, he didn't know. Maybe someday. But after the initial head slam, he'd replayed the woman's words over and over in his head until they'd stopped reverberating enough for him to actually hear what she was saying. And to realize she was right. About a lot of things. Not the least of which was that he'd apparently gotten the wrong end of the stick about this being-a-man business. No matter how honorable his intentions.

Because, truth? His releasing Kelly had been far more about saving his own hide than hers.

Matt took a deep breath, then Kelly's hand, pocketing it between both of his. "Got a minute?"

She leaned into his shoulder. "As many as you want. I'm not going anywhere."

His heart thumping, Matt kissed her hair, then whispered, "What I said earlier about not letting you go just because you're scared? What I probably should have said was—" his chest cramped "—that I'm not letting you go just because *I* am."

For a moment, she simply stroked his forearm with one fingertip, then lifted her head to look into his eyes. "Of?"

It surprised him that even after all the soul-searching, the answer still caught in his throat. That exactly like so many of those people he'd interviewed over the course of his career, he'd have to circle around it, pounce when it—or he—wasn't looking. Catch the fear off guard.

He let go of Kelly's hand to lean forward, watching

some gal across the street plod barefoot across her yard to move her sprinkler—a simple, mundane act he found weirdly soothing.

"After my parents died," he said, "I was so…angry. At God, at the universe, whatever. Even at all those people who were only trying to be nice to me, for God's sake. But especially at my father, for making us get into that car when he was drunk—"

"Oh, honey… Sabrina never told me that."

"I don't think she knew. In fact, I don't think she was aware of…of a lot that had gone on. She was my father's little angel. Me—" he shoved out a sigh "—not so much. Anyway…by that point, I suppose I'd lost trust in whatever it was I was *supposed* to trust. Hell, I wouldn't even let Mom hug me. Never mind I wanted her to more than anything. Especially since I missed my own mother so damn much. But I guess, in my own little-kid way, I figured the only person I could count on was me." He smirked. "Sound familiar?"

"I wasn't six," Kelly said gently.

"True. But, looking back, I think that's when the protective thing kicked in. Starting with Bree, but God knows not ending there. Maybe…" He rubbed the side of his nose. "Maybe I thought if I was the one doing the protecting, I couldn't be hurt?"

And there it was, the splinter he'd refused to look at, let alone tried to yank out, for nearly thirty years.

Kelly pressed herself to his side. "So you toughed it out."

Matt laughed softly. "Actually, Mom—Jeanne—called me her little toughie. Always with a smile. And a kiss, whether I wanted it or not. Much, *much* later, she told me she'd refused to give up on me. To accept for a minute that I couldn't get past the pain." He paused. "All along, I had the perfect example right in front of me. In someone

I practically worshipped. Eventually, anyway. And yet…I couldn't hear what she was saying. Because I couldn't—or wouldn't—let her all the way in." A breath pushed through his lips. "Her, or anyone else."

"Matt…you're one of the most giving people I've ever met—"

"So are you. Yeah, you are," he said when she started to protest. "So no arguments. But accepting's just as important, isn't it? It's about—" he made a weighing motion with his hands "—balance. Like you said. Not just honesty, but *trust.* And I had no right, none, to accuse you of holding back when I was doing the same damn thing. Maybe for different reasons, maybe I didn't even fully realize I was doing it, but the result was the same." He paused, then said, "Marcia wasn't worth fighting for. You are. But I can't do that while I'm busy watching my own back." At her silence, he looked over. "No comment?"

Mimicking his pose, Kelly sat forward, their thighs touching. "So…it wasn't just me?"

Matt wagged his head. "Oh, hell, no." His eyes cut to the side of his face. "That make you feel better?"

"Actually…yeah." She smiled. "Thank you."

"You're welcome—"

"Although I was totally prepared to prostrate myself at your feet and beg you to take me back—"

"Really."

"Pretty much. But the mutual groveling thing works, too. I…cleared a lot of junk out of my head, too. Feels a *lot* lighter in there," she said with a soft laugh. A breeze caught the ends of her hair, blowing it across his arm. "So…where do we go from here?"

"I suppose…wherever we want."

A neighbor's orange tabby stalked into the yard, realized they were sitting there and streaked off again. Kelly laughed. "It's really dumb, isn't it? To cut yourself off because of what you're afraid *might* happen?"

"Yeah," Matt sighed out. "It really is."

For a long moment they just sat there, listening to the chirping birds and the kids' laughter coming through the open window, the buzz of a little twin-engine plane circling overhead. Then Kelly reached over and took his hand. "I won't ever leave you, Matt. I promise. Even if I'm scared."

"Glad to hear it. Because I won't let you. Even if I am."

"So—" she cocked her head, smiling at him "—we're good?"

Over the rush of blood in his ears, Matt slung an arm around her shoulders, pulled her close and plunged. "I'm not saying I'm done making mistakes, but I sure as hell am not about to make this one again. I'm in this for the long haul, babe. As completely as I know how. No more half-assed let's-see-where-this-goes, no more escape clauses or ass covering. I'm here for *you*. For *us*. Whatever comes up… We'll get through it together."

Grinning, he leaned closer and whispered, "The only space I'm planning on giving you is next to me. In my bed. My life. Meaning I'm putting it right out there, right now, that in my mind there's only one possible outcome for this, and that's us getting married. Not like next week or anything, but—"

"Yes," Kelly said, and Matt stopped, mouth open. Then his brows flew up.

"Really?"

"You got a better idea?"

"Hell, no," he said, and kissed her, and again for good measure…and her smile, when he lifted his mouth from hers, swept away every last trace of fear, and doubt, and loneliness.

For good.

Epilogue

"So let me get a good look at this thing," Sabrina said, planting her skinny tush next to Kelly on the Colonel's porch swing, then grabbing Kelly's left hand. In the fading June light, the perfect little ruby looked even redder, the tiny diamonds encircling the oval stone twinkling like mad. "Ooh, pretty. And Matt really picked it out all by himself?"

Kelly laughed. "Sort of. I might've worked my thing for rubies into the conversation a time or two."

Matt's twin chuckled, then let go of Kelly's hand to lean her head against her shoulder, like they used to do when they'd been kids, shoving the heel of her red leather flat against the floorboard to set the swing in motion. Laughter filtered out from behind the house, where the Colonel's seventieth birthday bash was drawing to a close, and Bree sighed.

"I don't know which of you I'm happier for," she said.

"You or Matty. Actually—" she sat up again "—I take that back. I'm happiest for me, because..." She pressed a hand to her chest, tears shining in her eyes. "Because I don't have to choose between you."

Laughing, Kelly sucked in a deep, contented breath that smelled of Bree's designer perfume, of Jeanne's fragrant roses smothering the front of the house. Their friendship as fully in bloom again as those roses, it seemed as though the intervening years had never happened. In fact, Bree had asked Kelly to be her matron of honor for her hotsy-totsy Long Island wedding a year hence. An honor Kelly readily accepted, but only if Sabrina returned the favor by agreeing to be Kelly's only attendant, at this very house in six weeks' time.

A thought that sent a little thrill scooting up Kelly's spine...especially when Matt appeared at the front door, shaking his head at the two of them. Her angel, most definitely. But an angel there for *her,* not who he needed her to be to bolster his own ego. An angel who supported her, cheered for her and, yes, would protect her and her children with everything he had in him...but whose love made her *more,* not less.

And Kelly would do no less for him.

"You might want to get back there," Matt said with a grin for his sister, "before the others eat your fiancé alive."

"Oh, gawd," she said, patting Kelly's knee before propelling herself off the swing, down the stairs and around the side of the house, bellowing, "Hey! You guys! Be nice...." and Kelly thought, *God, I love these people.*

Her people now. For reals, as Coop would say.

The swing shuddered, making the loose ends of the chain jangle when Matt lowered himself to it and draped an arm around Kelly's shoulders, and she sighed. For now—since they'd decided not to change living arrangements *again* until after the wedding—it was still about these stolen moments, each one precious, perfect, shimmering with the promise of forever.

"Mmm...you smell like a hamburger," she said, rubbing her nose in his T-shirt, and he chuckled. "Kids okay?"

"You kidding?" he said. "With Ethan's brood? They're in heaven."

Kelly smiled, thinking how a few months ago she could have never imagined any of this. That she'd be back in Maple River, that Coop would blossom into the self-assured kid he'd become, confident in not just his abilities, but most important, in who he was. That the brooding, dark-eyed boy she'd crushed on all those years ago would end up being her Mr. Right after all. And right on time.

And right on cue, Matt picked up her left hand, toyed with the ring and murmured, "And yourself?" as he placed a soft kiss in her hair. "How're you doing?"

"You have to ask?" she said with a smile, lifting her face for a real kiss. Then, releasing another breath, she snuggled close again, letting happiness wash over her. Through her.

Because maybe their pasts had been crazy and scrambled and, sometimes, not so hot. But right now?

Perfect didn't even begin to cover it.

* * * * *

COMING NEXT MONTH FROM

HARLEQUIN®

SPECIAL EDITION

Available February 18, 2014

#2317 LASSOED BY FORTUNE

The Fortunes of Texas: Welcome to Horseback Hollow
by Marie Ferrarella

Liam Jones doesn't want any part of newfound Fortune relatives—or the changes they bring to Horseback Hollow. *He's crazy,* thinks Julia Tierney. The ambitious beauty was always the one Liam could never snag in high school. When Julia becomes the chef at a local restaurant, Julia and Liam find that old attractions die hard....

#2318 THE DADDY SECRET

Return to Brighton Valley • by Judy Duarte

When Mallory Dickinson gave up her son, she never thought she'd see Brighton Valley—or her baby's father, Rick Martinez—again. A decade later, she's back in town with her son, whom she adopted—and Rick's become a responsible veterinarian. Can the former bad boy and the social worker let their guards down to allow love in?

#2319 A PROPOSAL AT THE WEDDING

Bride Mountain • by Gina Wilkins

Father-of-the-bride Paul Brennan can't help but find himself tempted by irresistible innkeeper Bonnie Carmichael. Trouble arises, though, since Bonnie hopes to create a life and family at Bride Mountain Inn, and Paul's already done fatherhood. In the shadow of Bride Mountain, love blooms as they find their way to a happily-ever-after.

#2320 FINDING FAMILY...AND FOREVER?

The Bachelors of Blackwater Lake • by Teresa Southwick

Kidnapped as a child, Emma Robbins heads to Blackwater Lake to find her birth family. In the process, she becomes the nanny to Dr. Justin Flint's young son. The handsome widower is unwillingly attracted to the lovely newcomer, who loves the boy as her own, but secrets and lies may undermine the family they begin to build.

#2321 HER ACCIDENTAL ENGAGEMENT • by Michelle Major

Single mom Julia Morgan needs a man—not for love, but to keep custody of her son, Charlie. Local police chief Sam Callahan wants to keep his family out of his love life. The two engage in a romance of convenience, but what begins as a pretense might just evolve into true love.

#2322 THE ONE HE'S BEEN LOOKING FOR • by Joanna Sims

World-renowned photographer Ian Sterling is going blind, and he wants to find the model of his dreams before he loses his sight entirely. He finds his muse in rebellious Jordan Brand, but there's more than a camera between these two. To truly heal, Ian must open his heart to see what's been in front of him all along.

YOU CAN FIND MORE INFORMATION ON UPCOMING HARLEQUIN® TITLES, FREE EXCERPTS AND MORE AT WWW.HARLEQUIN.COM.

HSECNM0214

When Mallory Dickinson is reunited with her first love, she has to decide whether to tell him her deepest secret—that her young son is his biological child!

***

Mallory took a deep breath, probably trying to gather her thoughts—or maybe to lie.

But it didn't take a brain surgeon to see the truth. She'd kept the baby she was supposed to have given up for adoption, and she'd let ten years go by without telling Rick.

Betrayal gnawed at his gut.

"Lucas called you a doctor," she said, arching a delicate brow.

"I'm a veterinarian. My clinic is just down the street."

As she mulled that over, Lucas sidled up to Rick wearing a bright-eyed grin. "Did you come to ask my mom about Buddy?"

No, the dog was the last thing he'd come to talk to Mallory about. And while he hadn't been sure just how the conversation was going to unfold when he arrived, it had just taken a sudden and unexpected turn.

"Why would he come to talk to me about his dog?" Mallory asked her son.

Or rather *their* son. Who else could the boy be?

Lucas, who wore a smile that indicated he was completely oblivious to the tension building between the adults, approached Mallory. "Because Buddy needs a home. Since we have a yard now, can I have him? *Please?* I promise to take care of him and walk him and everything."

HSEEXP0214

She said, "We'll talk about it later."

"Okay. Thanks." He flashed Rick a smile, then turned and headed toward the stairs.

As Lucas was leaving, Rick's gaze traveled from the boy to Mallory and back again. Finally, when they were alone, Rick folded his arms across his chest, shifted his weight to one hip and smirked.

"Cute kid," he said.

Mallory flushed brighter still, and she wiped her palms along her hips.

Nervous, huh? Rick's internal B.S. detector slipped into overdrive.

Well, she ought to be.

When Rick had found out about her pregnancy, he'd been only seventeen, but he'd offered to quit school, get a job and marry her. However, her grandparents had decided that she was too young and convinced her that adoption was the only way to go. So they'd sent her to Boston to live with her aunt Carrie until the birth.

Yet in spite of what she'd promised him when she left, she hadn't come back to Brighton Valley. And within six months' time, he'd lost all contact with her—through no fault of his own.

Apparently, she'd had a change of heart about the adoption. And about the feelings she'd claimed she'd had for him, too.

***

Enjoy this sneak peek from USA TODAY *bestselling author Judy Duarte's THE DADDY SECRET, the first book in* RETURN TO BRIGHTON VALLEY, *a brand-new miniseries coming in March 2014!*

HSEEXP0214